THE FLOATING LEAF

THE FLOATING LEAF

Orange Books Publication

Smriti Nagar, Bhilai, Chhattisgarh - 490020

Website: **www.orangebooks.in**

First Edition, 2023

THE FLOATING LEAF

NEELANJANA BOSE

OrangeBooks Publication

www.orangebooks.in

With the blessings of Shirdi Sai Baba

'The Floating Leaf'

Is Dedicated To

" Memories are timeless treasures of the heart."
Photograph of Sobha & Lily in Rourkela, 1968.

Smt. **Sobha Ghosh,** my maternal grandmother, and Smt. **Lily De Sircar,** my mother. The two most awesome women in my life, who are no more, but are more alive in me than ever. We all share a mother-daughter-infinity bond.

Neelanjana Bose.

Acknowledgment

"There is no greater agony than bearing an untold story inside you"

Maya Angelou

I would like to acknowledge my mother Smt. Lily De Sircar, for her faith in me, that one day I would write this story for her.

My husband Mr. Sujeet Kumar Bose for his constant encouragement. My children Swapneel & Neelakshee for supporting me always. My brother-in-law Mr. Abhijeet Bannerjee for guiding me.

I am grateful to Orange Publication.in and the team for their help and support in every step.

Neelanjana Bose.

Author's Note

April 14, 2021, 10:30 p.m.

My RTPCR test report showed COVID positive.

I was rushed to a nearby hospital in an ambulance. I was feeling unwell, as if my lungs were being crushed. I was exhausted and just wanted to sleep.

The next four days, I was not well. Doctors and nurses came, and I was given so many medicines and put on drips. In my delirious state, they appeared as aliens to me with their protective gear, masks, and huge magnified specs.

On the fifth day, I felt better. I could register my surroundings and hear the chaos in the hospital as people were brought in critical condition. People were moaning, crying, and dying. Nurses and doctors were rushing around.

It was during these eight days at the hospital that I realised that I could have died of COVID, and if I had, what would I have regretted the most?

The first on my list was losing my blessed life and my loving family. I almost had tears in my eyes, thinking of my family without me. But then my logical sense took over, and I thought of the second important thing I would regret not doing.

"Writing my grandmother's life story"

On a sultry summer afternoon in 1986, when I was in the 7th grade, my mother started telling me my grandmother's real-life experiences and stories. I was intrigued.

A week later, when she had completed the story, my mother told me, "You must write your grandmother's story as a tribute to her."

I promised her that I would do so, but as life took its turn and I went along with its flow, I pushed this story somewhere at the back of my mind.

That day, on the hospital bed, I decided to fulfil my promise to my mother.

Here I am with my grandmother's story, "The Floating Leaf."

' The Floating Leaf 'depicts the 1940s era. The incidents, political upheavals, and outcomes have been researched from various online sources. I do not claim the correctness of the historical facts of the story. Many parts have been fictionalized by me, so any resemblance to living or dead characters is purely coincidental.

Neelanjana Bose

Content

PROLOGUE

In the 1940s, India was brimming with political, social, and religious upheavals. It was a time of transition from Colonial India to Independent India. Almost two centuries of atrocious and manipulative British rule had pushed the educated Indians and the common masses against the wall. It was only a matter of time, that India would be free from the colonial rule.

Netaji Subhas Chandra Bose had raised Azad Hind Fauz with the help of the Japanese, Indian soldiers working under the British army had joined the Indian Nation Army to fight against the British. Netaji believed that if Indians were united, British Colonialism would end.

Gandhiji on the other hand, had started the Quit India Movement. He introduced the Satyagraha movement and inspired Indians to defy British rule through non-violent ways. He wanted to appeal to the goodness of the rulers to get freedom for India.

The British Raj was already reeling under the effects of World War II, at the end of the war they were left to rule India with some 40,000 British soldiers and some 2.5 million Indian soldiers. The Britishers were aware of the discontent of the Indian soldiers, the formation of the Indian National Army under Subhas Chandra Bose had shaken them, and the uprising of the Royal Indian Navy made things worse. The British knew they could not rule India without the support of the Indians, as they had done in the past nearly 200 years. They realized that Indians have arisen to their right to freedom and time had come for them to retreat.

The British Empire thrived on the policy of Divide and rule in India. When they realized that the time has come for them to end their rule, they played their ultimate trick to divide the people of India based on their religion. They planted the seed of animosity between the Hindus and Muslims of India. The British decided to partition the country and give Pakistan to the Muslims. Thus, began a series of Hindu -Muslim riots all around India. The most violent riots of 1946 in Calcutta resulted in thousands of deaths and lakhs of people were left wounded and homeless. After Indian Independence Bill was passed in 1947, began history's most heart- wrenching blood-stained exodus was faced by the Hindus and Muslims who were forced to move from their birthplace to their respective countries of choice, as set by the British Raj. Seven decades later the hatred is still evident.

 The Indian Society in the 1940s was filled with chaos and corruption. Women bore the brunt of the evilness of the society. Whether be the Mughal invaders, the British, or the rules of the patriarchal society, the women were mistreated, tortured, and got a raw deal. Though the British had formed laws and had abolished many inhumane social evils prevalent in Indian society like the Sati System, Child marriage, and Purdah System, these social evils still thrived in society. The majority of the population was uneducated. So, gender discrimination against women continued in various forms, inside and outside the house.

Such were the times when my story begins…. It would be better to say my grandmother Sova's story begins….

Chapter 1

SOVA

Sova was 15, quite tall for her age, with knee-length jet-black neatly plaited hair. She draped her cotton saree perfectly; it complimented her slender figure well. Her sparkling eyes created an aura of wonderment. She was an ardent reader, she loved being lost in the world of books. She journeyed through many lands, kingdoms, and universes through her books. Her horizons were broadened and her thoughts and ideas were very revolutionary and advanced in comparison to girls of her age. She was the only child of her parents. Her father worked in the Indian Railways. Her mother, Maya Devi was a social worker, she had ensured Sova completed high school and was well-versed in sewing, stitching, and embroidery. Sova was also an excellent cook, like her mother. They lived in Barakhamba Road in the Railway quarters in Delhi. Sova was well-loved by everyone in her colony, as she was generous and helpful by nature.

Sova loved writing everyday events that were worth remembering in her diary. Every night she would sit down to pen her thoughts in her little red diary.

16th Oct 1940, 8:30 pm

My marriage has been fixed with Nalin Kanti Ghosh of Calcutta. He works as a clerk in the Post office. Ma said, "They are a well-to-do family". Nalin's father is the Director General of Telephones in the Northern Region. Ma says Mr. Ghosh's sister had seen me when I had gone to my friend Nutan's house after my high school exams. I had not noticed her then. Nutan had said her father's friend's sister from Calcutta was visiting them. Later she met my Baba and my marriage had been fixed with her eldest nephew. I don't know what to feel to be happy…sad…to worry…or to be frightened.

Nalin came to see me on 15th October. He is a shy person. He is not very tall. He looked studious with his specs and funny hair. Ma says he is 5 years older than me, still a boy …in due time he will look mature like a man. He looked better than Shanti's husband, I feel bad for Shanti. Her father married her to a widower because he was ready to marry without a dowry.

Shanti was crying bitterly. I pray for a good life after marriage and hope Nalin turns out to be a good person.

On 5th November 1940, Sova was set to marry Nalin Kanti Ghosh. A month prior to her wedding Sova's maternal uncle and aunt, her maternal grandparents, and a few relatives had arrived to prepare for the wedding. Sova stayed back home while her parents and relatives went shopping for her sarees, jewelry, and other gifts. In those days, girls were not allowed to choose their own trousseau, it was considered inappropriate for a girl to be so enthusiastic about her own marriage. The elderly women and relatives decided what was best for the young bride. Sova was not interested in such things as well, what brightened her eyes with excitement were books and her father who worked in the Railways ensured he brought her many books to read from the Wheeler company bookstores in Delhi Railway station.

The caterer was booked, the marriage venue was arranged and Sova's father ensured good arrangements for the bridegroom's friends and relatives, as they were the elites of Calcutta.

On 3rd of November, Sova's house was filled with relatives. Many of them she hardly recognized, and many others she was getting acquainted with for the very first time. All were in a great mood. The women were chatting and busy preparing for the rituals. Bengali marriages are very elaborate, many rituals are customized for the fun and entertainment of the relatives and friends. The children from her neighborhood were super excited that their Sova Didi was getting married, along with her distant cousin's children, who were all running around gleefully, often being reprimanded for causing chaos. The men were busy doing nothing much except resting or chatting, asking for tea for fueling themselves up.

The women on the other hand were all busy either tending to their male relatives and the children's demands for eatables or cups of tea, at the same time helping to arrange the various rituals necessary for the wedding. The married women were busy making the 'SHREE' which symbolizes Goddess Lakshmi, the goddess of wealth and prosperity. The 'SHREE' is a pyramid-like structure made of rice flour dough, turmeric, and vermillion, kneaded in mustard oil to make it clay-like and then creatively decorated. The main aim is to ensure the 'SHREE' retains its shape and beauty all through the marriage ceremonies, ensuring the goddess's blessing at all times.

On the 4th of November, "Nandi Mukh", another important ritual was performed, whereby the deceased ancestors are worshipped, seeking their blessing for the marriage. This is followed by the ritualistic "Aieburo Bhat" symbolizing the last meal before tying the knot. Sova had read about marriages in books and had attended her cousin's marriage a few years back but this experience was daunting. So many people were giving her so many instructions, pulling her leg, and enjoying themselves. Sova allowed herself to be drawn into the festive atmosphere though she was scared deep within. She was given a somewhat broad idea as to what to expect after marriage by her mother and aunt, both seemed quite uncomfortable to discuss sex with her. Sex has always been a taboo in India and Indians avoid discussing it altogether. So, the information Sova got was obscure and it baffled her.

As Sova sat to eat her last meal as an unmarried girl, she was mesmerized to see the huge bronze plate filled with delicious platter of food items and some eight-bronze bowls filled with sweets, puddings and curries. Sova's sisters were waiting for their turn to share the food from her plate as it was assumed that if they ate from her plate, they would be the next to get married. The fun and excitement of the wedding was catching up as more of her relatives kept pouring in from different parts of the country.

On the morning of 5th of November, the day of Sova's marriage, the groom's family members came with numerous gifts in beautifully decorated boxes, sarees wrapped artistically into different shapes, toiletries, jewelry, and the best of Bengali sweets from Calcutta for the bride and her family. The turmeric paste brought by them was used for Sova's Haldi ceremony. In Haldi Ceremony, the turmeric paste brought by the groom's family is applied to the bride by all her relatives, this gives an ultra-glow to the bride on her special night. To make it more fun the relatives smear the turmeric paste on each other and ensure they glow at the wedding ceremony, as well.

In the evening, Sova dressed as a bride looked beautiful in the red-colored Benarasi saree draped to perfection.

The gold ornaments glittered on her and her tall slenderness made her look like an 'Apsara', the celestial beauty. The marriage ceremony was longer in duration as Sanskrit shlokas filled the night air, the vibrations of the mantras were meant to seal the marital union for life. Sova was married to Nalin. By the time the bride and the groom could have their dinner, it was quite late in the night. The next few hours up until dawn was spent by both Sova and Nalin's cousins and relatives, singing Rabindra sangeet, dancing, and getting to know each other well. It is believed that a newly wedded couple must not sleep on their wedding night, to ensure a blissful union. This belief prevents the couples to doze off, while their relatives have great fun keeping them awake by entertaining them.

Early the next morning Sova's mother and other elders started the rest of the rituals for the departure of Sova to her new family in Calcutta, this ritual is called 'Bidaai', the farewell. A girl tended with love and care is sent off to her new home, to a new environment by her parents after marriage. This ritual left Sova's parents in tears as they realized they would not be able to see her or hear her sweet voice every day. They would have to learn to live their lives without her. Teary-eyed Sova bid goodbye to her parents and boarded the train with her husband and his relatives. It was two days of journey by train to reach Calcutta.

As their car was passing through the Howrah Bridge, Sova could see the river Ganga flowing below. She joined her hands in reverence to the great river. The black and yellow cabs were zooming past them, there were crowded buses and hundreds of humans hurrying to their destined destination with determination. Sova was soaking in the city's pulse, she had read about this great city and the great men of this city who have made the country so proud. For the first, time she felt a strange joy and excitement at the thought of exploring this great city.

The car moved into the residential area, and Sova noticed beautifully designed bungalows, evidence of British influence in architecture. As the car halted at the driveway, Sova saw her new house for the first time. A huge white and red three-storied mansion, a neatly maintained garden with rose bushes along the driveway. A broad stairway leading up to a semicircular columned verandah gave a very elegant look to the house. It reminded Sova of government guest houses she had seen in Delhi. Sova wanted to have a good look but she was ushered into one of the rooms and many ladies took charge of her, ensuring she is bathed, dressed, and ready for a number of rituals for the rest of the day. In the midst of all the dressing ups, and meeting scores of new relatives of Nalin, Sova was supposed to remember her relation to each one of them and address them accordingly. Being a girl of calm demeanor Sova took it up as a challenge to remember most of the relatives and their names. Whenever she needed help Nalin's younger siblings Saikat and Anjana would readily help. In the first few days, Sova created a strong bond with Nalin's siblings.

Sova slowly started adjusting to her new life, new surroundings, and new family. She had always been an observant girl, this helped her. At times she would yearn for her mother's loving touch and her father's care but then she was learning how to live without them.

Saikat and Anjana would accompany Sova to explore the house and often play hide and seek, on their way around. Sova felt very comfortable with the children, as she was just a few years older than them.

Sova was impressed with the number of servants present in her in-law's house. The servants would appear like Jinns (spirits) before she could put her empty cup on the table, to take it away. Sova was not expected to cook but just direct the elderly maid Dhanoi about the lunch and dinner menu. Dhanoi had been working in the household for many years and was not very happy to be instructed by a young girl, she made it very evident within a few days to Sova. Sova respected her authority and stepped back. Nalin's aunt was a good lady, she helped Sova settle down to her new life. Sova had heard about 'TELEPHONES' but saw and learned to use it in her new house. Nalin taught her how to receive calls and how to book a call. All these new experiences were very exciting for Sova. She could have assumed herself very lucky but for one thing. The only person who seemed unapproachable and distant towards her was her father-in-law. Sova was puzzled by his rude behavior towards her and Nalin, but she didn't have the courage to ask anyone about it, even Nalin seemed unaware of her plight.

Two months after marriage Sova made the next entry in her Red Diary.

15th January 1941, 2:15 pm

I have been married for two months now. I am still adjusting to my new life. Nalin is a good man, very understanding. He has told me to continue my studies. He said he would enroll me as a private student and I need to go just to give my Higher secondary exam, I needn't go to school. He is very kind but my father-in-law Rai Saheb, is such a strange man. I think he hates me. Whenever he sees me and Nalin together, he gets angry and starts rebuking Nalin for no reason. I feel bad for Nalin.

I used a telephone for the very first time. Nalin dialed some number and the operator connected me to my father's office in Delhi Railways headquarters. Baba started crying hearing my voice. I too cried and couldn't say much. A telephone is so useful.

5th February 1941 ,9:30 pm

Dhanoi, the old maidservant of the house is not a good person. Though she is just a servant my father-in-law gives her too much importance. She always tries to put me down in front of others. I feel bad for Saikat and Anjana. They are so young and are growing up without their mother's love and affection, always reprimanded by their father for small mistakes.

7th May 1941, 5:00pm

Yesterday Nalin was very excited. He told me he would take me to see a movie. I was not willing as I know how my father-in-law always reacts if he sees me and Nalin together. I didn't want any disturbance in the household. But Nalin said his father's job as the Director General of

Telephones, requires him to stay in Calcutta for 6 months and in Delhi for the rest of the 6 months.

I am unsure whether to be excited or not, but thinking of 6 months without witnessing the meaningless scolding, abusing the servants for no reason, constant negativity .... I could live without all that...peacefully. I am sure Lord Krishna has a hand in making my life a little better.

Sova had an amazing time for 6 months when her father-in-law was in Delhi. Nalin would take her to movies on Sundays, sometimes they would end up watching all three shows in the movie theatre. They would stroll along the banks of river Hooghly or go boating in the evenings after Nalin returned from his work. Mostly they ate outside and returned home late. No one would say a thing. Dhanoi the old maid would sneer from behind but say nothing in front of them. The honeymoon period of Sova and Nalin, made them realize that they were soul mates.

Six months later, Sova's father-in-law the 'Rai Saheb' (Rai Saheb was the title conferred to those Indians whom the British favored and held high posts in their government) returned back to Calcutta. With him came the toxic atmosphere. Everyone in the household lived in fear in his presence. Rai Saheb's younger brothers had partitioned their ancestral property and rarely interacted with their older brother because of his rude behavior and rotten temperament. Though they loved Sova and bonded with her well in their elder brother's absence. During such times, Nalin would go into a shell and all the outings and fun time would cease. Sova engaged herself in taking care of Nalin's siblings and spent most of her time with them. She would keep herself busy teaching them and continued reading a lot. Within a few months of marriage Sova had won over everyone's heart, except her father-in-law and the old maid Dhanoi.

Chapter 2

The Peer Baba

One evening, Dhanoi had gone for some errand and had not returned. It was getting dark so Sova decided to tell the cook to prepare for dinner. The cook informed her that the cooking oil was in the store room and they were not allowed to enter until Dhanoi came. Sova felt irritated by the fact that Dhanoi was acting as the master of the house, with her highhanded ways. Sova decided to get the cooking oil from the store room herself. She took the store room keys and walked towards the courtyard; the store room was located midway between the landing of the staircase of the inner courtyard. As she unlocked the door and went inside the room, she remembered something

Dhanoi had told her when she had first met her. "Never enter the store room when you are dirty or mensurating or without taking a bath. You will repent" Dhanoi had spoken sternly, rounding her eyes, warningly at Sova. Sova stood undecidedly whether to search for the oil can or walk out of the room. She was about to walk away when she saw the oil can on the shelf. She took the oil can, quietly closed the door behind her and decided not speak about this incident to Dhanoi. Sova handed over the oil can to the cook and instructed her on the dinner menu and returned to her room.

The next afternoon after lunch, Sova went to her room. She closed her bedroom door and laid down for her afternoon siesta. Having had a lunch of rice and poppy seed curry, a lethal combination for deep sleep soon Sova was in a semi-conscious state, she was asleep but she could see her room clearly. Her eyes fixed on the door and in her sleep, she could see it was opening slowly. She could feel cool air entering through the open door of her room, her spine chilled and she could feel goosebumps on her body. She was in a trance-like state. Through her partially closed eyelids, she saw a very tall man entering her room. She tried to look at the face but couldn't see as the man was too tall. Sova was unable to move, her limbs were immobile. She wanted to open her eyes wide to see who the man was but her body seemed to be paralyzed. She could feel her scream stifling in her throat. She seemed to struggle to come out of her dream but she couldn't…she felt trapped. The tall figure came nearer and nearer to her bed and then slowly started bending down towards her…at one point she could feel the man's breath over her face, her heart started sinking in fear…Sova's eyes were wide open but she could see nothing, her eyes were filled with watery fluid… tears had built up in her eyes and then suddenly everything became black.

Sova woke up with a splitting headache and she felt very uncomfortable. Sova lay on her bed for quite some time trying to understand …whether it was a real incident or was it a dream …. had she seen a nightmare…. who was the tall man…she checked the clock; she had been sleeping for 5 hours. Something very rare because she rarely slept in the afternoons. As she sat on the bed, she was surprised to see the bedroom door wide open, she remembered locking it before going to bed. Sova felt confused. She had this feeling someone had entered her room when she was asleep.

By 6:30 pm Nalin came back from work and saw Sova sitting on the bed with a perplexed expression. He asked her and then Sova narrated to him the incident and the strange feeling of fear she was experiencing because of her dream. Nalin looked at her with a somber expression and said "Can you bring tea for me". Sova nodded and went to the kitchen. By the time she returned with his tea and snacks, Nalin had changed into his house clothes, sipping his tea asked her casually- "Did you enter the storeroom, without taking a bath today?" Sova looked at him surprised and nodded saying "Yesterday evening, I went to fetch the oil can, I was unclean" Nalin nodded and said "Well, it would seem strange but did you see a very tall man?" Again, Sova frowned and nodded. Clearing his throat Nalin spoke somberly, "There is a grave of a

Muslim priest (Peer Baba) under the storeroom floor. This is not the first time, whoever enters the room unclean, sees the Peer Baba. He has been seen by many of us, it's a fact that the room is haunted. I am sure you will be careful henceforth." Sova sat stupefied by that piece of information. She had thought she might have dreamt of the man but now she realized the dream was too real and as vivid as seeing something with open eyes. She promised herself to be very careful in the future so as not to annoy the dead and also, she was petrified at the thought of a haunted room.

Diary Entry 12th October 1941, 16:30

I am feeling quite uneasy after the store room incident. Nalin said the store room was haunted but I do not believe in ghosts. It is only our minds playing tricks…. but then so many people have seen the Baba…. all can't be hallucinating or were in a trance…I need to find out…do spirits exist?

Sova was deeply affected by the Peer Baba episode. She had read about ghosts, and supernatural beings in her story books. Never in her wildest dreams had she thought she would ever experience such an episode in real life. Ghosts, supernatural beings, and sightings have always been an important part of folklore and stories in Bengal, Sova had heard from her grandmother many ghost stories. It is generally the ghost stories that induced fear and sleep in young children on sultry summer afternoons. Every Bengali child is aware of the different types of ghosts, who would appear to rip them off if they didn't eat food, sleep on time, or did mischief. The ghosts were every parent and grandparents' tool to bring in some discipline and instill fear in children in those days.

Ghosts are called "Bhoot". The very word invokes fear among children. There are various forms of 'Bhoots' according to their gender and characteristics. A "Petni " is a female ghost who is unmarried and has some unfulfilled desires. The "Petnis" live in trees and attack passersby who disturb them. Whereas "Shankchunni" were married female ghosts who wear conch-shell bangles called "Sankha" which are worn by married women. Black magic was very popular in rural Bengal in those times and Tantrics were ascetic yogis who dedicated their lives to learning black magic by invoking the dead spirits. Such Tantrics had the power to invoke these spirits for either causing harm to enemies or for superstitious purposes. Then there was the "Brahmodaittyo", the most popular of all kinds of ghosts in Bengal. It was believed to be the ghost of a Brahmin. He was supposed to be a benevolent ghost, kind and helpful. There was "Nishi meaning the night. The night ghosts would call one's name at night. Whoever responded, his soul would get transferred into the Nishi ghosts through his voice. At night children would go off to sleep in fear that they might hear their names being called by the night ghost. There were a dozen types of ghosts in Bengali folklore. In an era when there were limited means of entertainment, these stories of ghosts and supernatural beings were quite popular.

Sova was curious about the Peer Baba incident, whom she had seen in her sleep or in her trans-like state. She went to the servants; the servants were tight-lipped and denied knowing anything. She understood they had been warned not to spread rumors about the hauntings.

One afternoon when everyone had retired for the afternoon siesta, Sova decided to visit Nalin's aunt Aruna who lived in the other part of the ancestral house and did not mingle with Sova's family. Sova had heard that Rai Saheb, her father-in-law had once insulted his younger brother Ronit Kanti and after that, both brothers were not on speaking terms. Sova knew she had to go to the aunt's house without being noticed by anyone, so she chose to go in the afternoon.

"Come Sova, come in", Aruna aunty welcomed her enthusiastically. She was a beautiful lady. In her late 30s, she wore a comfortable saree and was chewing betel leaves, which meant she had just had her lunch. She had two sons who were in school and her husband worked in the Indian Press, he generally returned home by 8 pm in the evening. Sova got comfortable in the charpoy, tucking the pillow on her lap. Aruna too laid down on the adjacent charpoy.

"Tell me, pretty girl, what brings you here?" she inquired. Sova smiled shyly and narrated the store room incident and the fearful dream. Aruna looked concerned, she pondered for some time then said "An incident occurred many years back. Are you sure you won't get perturbed by the story. This is not for the frail-hearted, dear". Aruna was trying to create an atmosphere of eeriness. Sova said innocently, "My Ma has told me, the only beings one needs to be frightened of, are the humans. Inside a human's mind dwells all kinds of notoriety…. we can be demons or Gods…good or bad souls…. it's all up to us."

Aruna cleared her throat and nodded in agreement and said "Very true".

"This land on which our house is built was bought by Nalin's great-grandfather long back. But was left abandoned for years altogether. A poor Muslim Peer Baba had built his hut on this land and lived there. Since no one came to claim this land, the Peer Baba continued staying in the hut. In the year 1925, Nalin's grandfather and Rai Saheb decided to build a big house where all of us could stay together. When they came to claim the land, they saw the old Peer Baba staying there. He was quite ill and was almost on his deathbed. They asked him to move but he denied saying they should wait for a few more days until his death. But Rai Saheb, you know is a strict man. He abused the Peer Baba, threatened to call the police, and asked the laborers to throw the old man out from his land.", Aruna paused to gauze Sova's reaction. Sova was frowning while mentally visualizing the scene. Aruna continued, "The architect of the house Madhusudan said that he would take care of the Peer Baba and no one needed to worry. So, the entire episode was forgotten as time passed and the huge palatial house was completed in three years' time." Aruna paused.

Sova sat upright, "Then…. then what happened…?", she asked curiously.

Aruna smiled and continued, "It was the housewarming celebration, prayers, and Sanskrit shlokas were being chanted by the Brahmin priests in the house. The room near the staircase landing was used as a store room, all the servants were moving in and out of the room, to get the provisions as and when required. Some 300 people were invited to have dinner on this occasion. The house was beautifully decorated. It was a festive atmosphere. By the time the guests left after dinner, it was almost 12:30 am. Soon we all retired to our rooms to sleep. The servants went to the terrace at the top of the building to sleep. Some extra helping hands and cooks had been hired to help. All of them were sleeping on the terrace like logs from the day's hard work." Aruna paused to put the betel leaf in her mouth. Her mouth was blood red as she was chewing the betel leaf, she looked quite mysteriously beautiful as she continued her narration.

"I am not sure of the exact time but suddenly we heard a lot of commotion… slowly the sound kept increasing…as if a group of people were screaming together. We all woke up alarmed, groggy …it must have been 2:30 -3:00 am in the morning.Ronit along with Rai Saheb and a few other relatives went upstairs to the terrace from where the noises were coming. When they reached the terrace, they stood stunned…the servants were tossing and turning, falling from one side to the other as if someone was beating them up mercilessly."

Sova had a horrified expression on her face as she was visualizing the event mentally. Seeing Sova's terrified expression, Aruna was pleased with her storytelling skills. She gently spat the red-colored liquid into a delicate brass container meant for the purpose and continued, "Seeing them screaming in pain, jostling from one side to other, Rai Saheb came to the conclusion that they must have consumed some plant drug which was why they were reacting in that way. He scolded them in a loud voice but they were screaming their lungs out in pain. This continued for some 30 mins after which…most of the servants fell to the ground exhausted, crying in pain. The commotion ceased. Everyone returned to their rooms. Rai Saheb was determined to send the servants to the police for creating a ruckus at night after consuming some unknown drugs."

"The Next morning when Dhanoi came to serve tea", Aruna paused, looking at the farthest corner of the room, as if recalling the incident of that day. "She had a red mark of a hand imprinted on her face. Her face was swollen and she looked really ill." "What happened Dhanoi…?" I asked her, surprised to see such a brutal mark on her face. Dhanoi was looking lost she muttered "I don't know lady, yesterday night suddenly I felt a big slap on my face as if someone had hit me with a plank. I think I passed out. This morning I saw this mark."

Aruna continued, "Rai Saheb called all the servants to meet him. When he saw them, he was speechless. They all had slap marks on their faces, backs, and legs. They were groaning in pain, looking really frightened." Sova knew the climax was nearing she also knew it was evening she had to return home but she couldn't leave without knowing the story till the end. Aruna sensed her dilemma and continued the narration cutting short many details. "What happened?" Rai Saheb had asked them rudely but with concern. One of the servants spoke, fear written all over his face, "Sahib, I saw a very tall man, …but later all I could feel was as if someone was beating me mercilessly…. see all these marks, they are hurting so much…." "What did you do….?" Rai Saheb himself sounded confused. These servants swayed their heads in denial, "Nothing wrong Saheb, we were working hard all day. Just rested half an hour in the store room, had betel leaf, bidi after lunch."

What Aruna missed telling Sova was many of the servants had spitted in the room while they were chewing the betel leaves. Rai Saheb dismissed them and called the architect Madhusudan and related the incident. Madhusudan looked quite nervous and then he said in a guilt-ridden voice "Rai Saheb, remember the Peer Baba who lived in this plot. At the time you asked me to build the house he died and he was buried in this plot by the Muslim neighbors. When I started the construction, the Muslim men warned me not to remove his grave because it might bring unrest to the departed soul. So, I built the store room over the grave. I thought in such a big house, a small room would be rarely used, I did not tell you all the details earlier on." Madhusudan paused guiltily, ready to hear abuses from Rai Saheb, but luckily Rai Saheb was lost in his thoughts. By afternoon, a few of the Muslim neighbors came to meet Rai Saheb when they heard of the incident. Old Maulvi, a teacher in the local Madrasa told "Please keep the room clean and ensure no one urinates, spits, or dirties the room. Peer Baba wants to rest in peace, allow him to. He will not harm anyone." Later Dhanoi had told the women of the house that she was having her periods and had entered the room many times.

It was thus clearly informed to all the members of the family, the servants, and cooks never to enter the room. Only Dhanoi, the maid would enter the room after bathing and the key would be with her. For a few years, everyone was very careful, and slowly everyone got accustomed to not entering the room. Only Dhanoi would clean it and enter whenever required. Whenever there were violations people would see the tall peer Baba, in a dream-like state.

As Sova returned to her room, she was very confused. She could visualize the night when the servants had been beaten up…no one knew who did it. "Was this story true" …she kept thinking of all possible reasons not to accept the fact that ghosts exist. She thought of her experience, it could be her guilty mind playing a trick on her…but then she never knew this story then. Later Sova converted the storeroom into the Pooja room, i.e., a room for worshipping. She would clean the room herself, light incense sticks, and enter only to worship. According to the Hindus, no one enters the worship room unclean, so both purposes were solved.

Diary Entry: 6th Feb 1942, 3:30 pm

Do I believe in supernatural beings? ghosts, evil sinister beings…. I am not sure. I feel some spirits are just trapped in this world unable to go to the other world due to some unfinished desires in life. In Delhi there was an incident of a newborn child whose mother had died at childbirth, the newborn would keep crying in spite of others feeding and caring for him. At midnight miraculously the baby would start giggling, looking at someone, and cooing happily as if it someone was near him. No one knew whom the baby saw, everyone said it was the mother who could not leave her newborn. These strange happenings are unexplained, the more we try to think logically the more confused we become.

Chapter 3

RAISAHEB: The Father-in-law

Rai Saheb Lalit Kanti was well known among his peers and colleagues as an extremely rude man with a foul temper. He held a high post in the British Government, the pride of the post and his own personal failings in life had turned him into an egoistic man. A man whom everyone respected only out of fear, not love.

After the brutal Jallianwala Bagh massacre in 1919, when British General Dyer opened fire on a crowd of unarmed Indian men, women and children who had gathered for Baisakhi (Spring festival) celebrations, firing 1600 rounds of ammunition. Some 10,000 people died as they could not escape the incessant firing. In spite of this brutality, General Dyer was not charged with murder by the British government, and Gandhiji in 1920, launched the Non-Violent, Non -Cooperation Movement against the British to demand for self-rule.

During this time, Lalit was pursuing his degree in science and it was in the college he had met Pramila, a feisty young girl who was outspoken, brave, and an excellent orator. Pramila's dad was a barrister, a renowned one. Students gathered to listen to her when she spoke about women's rights, patriarchy, and the unfair British rulers who turned blind eyes to the suffering of the Indians and sided with the murderers like Col. Dyer. Pramila was also a member of the Chatri Sangh (Female Student's Club). The Chatri Sangh was founded by Smt. Lila Roy a revolutionary activist and teacher. She encouraged girls to learn skills and handicrafts and be independent. By this time students all around the country were all gearing up for the Non-Cooperation movement and Pramila was one of them, leading the women.

Lalit had fallen in love with Pramila, though he never had the courage to tell her. After he completed his education and got a job in the Calcutta Telephone Company, he told his grandmother about Pramila. Very soon a proposal for marriage was sent to Pramila's house. Lalit was certain that being educated and in a good British government job would be enough for Pramila's dad to accept his proposal. But to his dismay, he was rejected by Pramila. She told him that she would not marry a person who worked for the British government. It was people like him, who were preventing Indians from getting freedom because they were helping the British to rule.

Lalit had felt the slap of her rejection hard on his cheeks and carried it as a reason to be rude and malicious towards one and all. His grandmother seeing his anger and frustrations had married him to a simple girl Dolon, a girl who would consider her husband her Devata, meaning GOD. Lalit vented out his anger and vengeance of rejection on the poor soul until she could not bear any more. She died leaving him with two sons and a daughter within 15 years of marriage.

Lalit was furious that his wife had left him alone, now he had no one to vent his anger upon. He spent his time and energy working day and night for the Calcutta Telephone Company. With years of dedicated hard work, the British government acknowledged him by awarding him the title of "RAISAHEB"

By the time Rai Saheb thought he had achieved his position in society and was thinking of remarrying, his eldest son Nalin turned 19, Nalin's marriage was fixed by Lalit's eldest sister, who lived with them and held a very respectable position in the household. Lalit was in his mid-40s. He wanted to protest and tell his sister that he was ready for second marriage. But Lalit's elder sister Mira Di knew his nature and she didn't want him to ruin another girl's life. She knew her brother was a heartless brute, who would marry only to torture a poor soul, as he had done to his first wife. Mira had taken care of all her brother's children when his wife had died, Lalit had never ever looked at them or cared for them. Remarrying her brother would mean more burden on her, so she smartly got the eldest son Nalin married, to put a stop to Lalit's dreams of remarrying.

This was the reason Lalit hated his eldest son Nalin and his beautiful bride Sova. He was a disillusioned man, a man who was consumed by his own anger. This story of her father-in-law's desire to remarry was not known to Sova when she had come as a young bride. If she would have known, she would have not felt so unloved and hated as she always felt in his presence. Even Nalin was unaware of the reason for his father's hatred towards him and his wife. Sometimes he used to guess that his father must be holding him responsible for his mother's death. He had asked Mira Aunty a few times in childhood "Why does Baba hate me?" Mira Aunty had avoided answering him saying "Your Baba is so busy with his work, he has no time, he loves all his children"

Once, after almost two years of marriage, Sova had asked Nalin innocently, "Did Baba (referring to her father-in-law) always behave this way with you?" Nalin had not bothered looking at Sova and had nodded his head. One evening after Nalin had just returned from the office and was washing his feet, Sova stood waiting for him on the stairs. Suddenly Rai Saheb had come out of his room, noticing the young couple looking at each other, a strange rage had shot up his brain. He had started abusing his son, calling him names 'Eunuch, a person without backbone, not a man enough.' etc. Nalin had stood near the stairs mortified in shame as Sova stood numbed by the vicious lashings of Rai Saheb. Later both returned to their room, unable to look at each other or speak. Late at night, Sova had told Nalin "I cannot have my child in such an atmosphere, I don't want my child to hear what I heard today". Nalin nodded and said "Don't worry, very soon we will move out of this house. I cannot bear it anymore"

The political scenario was taking a turn, Calcutta was the harbinger of change that the rest of India would face later. As time passed Sova realized that some people are born that way, they are born to torment others and the only way to escape their torment was to become invisible to them. At times she felt like a floating leaf which has fallen from its parent tree and is floating aimlessly around finding its own path in its own innocent ways, just like her. To avoid such feelings of rootlessness, such empty floating leaf-like feelings Sova submerged herself in her books and household chores. She started knitting wonderful sweaters for Nalin's siblings. She embroidered on bedsheets and made beautifully designed bedspreads. She spent the rest of her time reading books by the great writers Tolstoy, Rabindra Nath Tagore, and Bankim Chandra Chatterjee. The power of the pen aroused and stirred the masses and now India was on the verge of reclaiming its Independence from the British. Everyone was motivated to see India free from the clutches of British rule.

Chapter 4

The Week of the Long Knives

The year was 1945, five years had gone by, and Sobha turned twenty and conceived her first child. Nalin was over the moon. He knew it was time for him to take a major decision, which would create a lot of tension at home but it was for his own child's sake, he was determined to take this decision. He told Sova that he had already rented a house in the Bow Bazaar area of North Calcutta. Sova was worried, she knew hell would break loose once their decision to leave the ancestral house would be known to Rai Saheb.

As expected, when, Rai Saheb came to know his son was moving away to a separate rented house in North Calcutta, he chose his worst abuses and hurled them at his son and pregnant daughter -in-law. His last words were "Once you leave my house, you are no more related to me. I will never see your face ever again" The whole household had plunged into gloom. Saikat and Anjana, who loved Sova were weeping bitterly, they were losing a sister-in-law who loved them like a mother. Both Sova and Nalin left home teary-eyed but to a peaceful existence.

The house they moved to in Bow Bazaar belonged to a Bengali Brahmin gentleman Mr. Sukumar Bhattacharya. The house was three storied. On the ground floor lived Mr. Bhattacharya with his wife Shanti, two sons, and a daughter. The other two floors were given for rent. The first and the second floors were rented to two families each. The house was very big, rooms were massive with double-height ceilings. In summer the rooms were cooler. Long French windows ran into the common balcony where in the evenings Sova met the other tenants and chatted with them. Her neighbors and the landlady Mrs. Shanti Bhattacharya were all very helpful. On September 1945 Sova delivered a baby girl, to the joy of all her new neighbors. It was a happy time for Nalin and Sova and the baby girl nicknamed 'Khuku.' Khuku means a small girl.

In Bengal, every child is given a nickname which is quite embarrassing for the child later when the child grows up. But when they are kids such weird names suit them as parents call them lovingly. Nalin, Sova, and Khuku lived peacefully, far away from Rai Saheb and his house. Though Nalin had gone to give the news of his daughter's birth to his father, his father had not allowed him inside.

Nalin had decided not to mention this to Sova, as Sova would get emotional at such cruelty of her father-in-law.

Diary Entry: 15th March 1946 13:00 pm

British Prime Minister Clement Attlee has announced to start the process of transferring the administrative powers to the Indians. India is becoming free soon.

Diary Entry: 3 July 1946 4:00 pm

Khukhu is 10 months old now, she has learned to turn around, and she makes a lot of baby sounds as if talking to me. It is a boon to be a mother. I thank Lord Krishna for all his blessings on us.

Diary entry 29th July 1946 5:30 pm

Today is the first general strike in the Postal and Telegraph department. Nalin said this strike is the biggest general strike in the 200 years history of British rule over India. All Indians have united against the British. It is a big day, also Nalin is at home playing with Khuku. I have cooked his favorite Ilish fish curry. I feel so elated that we are on the verge of becoming a free country.

5th August 1946 4:15 pm

I am ill at ease with this news that the British Government in the process of transferring power has proposed to set up an interim government in India which would be represented by members of the Indian National Congress, the Muslim League, and other forces. These are presently the major political parties. The British Government has given the Indian National Congress one seat more than the Muslim League, so Muslim League leaders have rejected the proposal of an interim government. The Muslim League under Jinnah has passed a resolution in favor to establish Pakistan, a separate country for Muslims. The Muslim League leader Md Ali Jinnah has called on Muslims throughout India to observe "Direct Action Day" on 16th August. This is not a good situation. The British government had always used a divide-and-rule policy to rule India, now before leaving they are going to do worse, turning the Hindus and Muslims against each other. I am not feeling good about this…!

The announcement of the "Direct Action Day ", to be held on 16th August 1946 intensified a growing polarization between the two major political parties and the two major religious communities in India-The Hindus and Muslims. Chances of communal violence all around the country were very high. In Calcutta, the situation was particularly complex.

Since February 1946, there had been communal tension in Calcutta, these events were fanned up by the newspapers thereby increasing the antagonism between the two communities. The Muslim League chief minister of Bengal had advised the Governor of Bengal Sir Federick Burrows to declare a public holiday on 16th August, to minimize the risk of destruction to government offices, shops, and commercial buildings thus reducing risks of conflict. But Congress Party leaders accused the Muslim League government of promoting conflict by declaring a public holiday, which would mean all mischief makers would be free to take part in the protests and hartals, loot, and, destruction of public property easily.

The newspapers had published the itinerary for Direct Day Action. According to the itinerary complete hartal and general strike in all spheres of civic, commercial, and industrial life except essential services was declared. Processions from different parts of the city would meet at Shaheed Minar, where a joint mass rally would be held by the Chief Minister. The Direct-Action Day also coincided with the holy month of Ramzan, thus the leaders of the league used that to motivate the people to join the general strike by drawing a similarity between their protest with that of establishing a kingdom in heaven.

Certain Congress leaders too motivated the Hindus to rise with a strong sense of "Akhand Hindustan "(United India). They feared the Pakistani movement would outnumber them and would diminish their identity. Thus, the Congress leaders had asked the Hindu traders to open their businesses and not be a part of the strike. The British government was more concerned about protests which were aimed against them rather than the communal tension that was brewing between the two communities.

The Chief Minister of Bengal was a rival of Jinnah for the leadership of The Muslim League Party. In the year 1943, he had a major hand in the "Great Famine of Bengal" in which two to three million people died, the Hindus of Calcutta hated him. He was on the other hand idolized by the poor and uneducated Muslims. He had links with the Muslim underworld, which ran all illegal activities like gambling, smuggling, prostitution, etc. that had flourished in the port city so rampantly.

On 16th August 1946, what was supposed to be a peaceful demonstration as called by Jinnah, turned very ugly in

Calcutta, under the support of the Chief Minister. The Muslims took his support as an indication to teach a lesson to the Hindus. Thus, what followed was the merciless killing of the Hindus in Muslim -majority areas. What was surprising was the brutality that was used by the Muslims, this stunned the nation.

On 16th August 1946, Nalin left for his job at the post office. Post offices were open as it was considered to be essential services. Sova while packing the tiffin box had asked Nalin "Is it safe to go out today? The newspapers are warning that the protests will not be peaceful". Seeing the worried expression on Sova's face Nalin calmed her and said, "Don't worry, I will be inside the post office. In case of any unruly incident, we will close our doors. It has been advised by our Postmaster. We cannot allow mobsters to enter and destroy government property. I will be safe" He looked at her and added "You on the other hand, do not go out at all, not even to the neighboring shop, stay inside with Khuku. If too much trouble brews up, I might return home early". With these words Nalin had left for his office, pecking Khuku's forehead.

By afternoon, there was news of riots spreading throughout Calcutta. It started with Muslims forcing the Hindu shopkeepers to close their shops and the Hindus retaliated stopping the procession of the Muslim League. The Muslim League rally at Saheed Minar was the largest Muslim assembly and, in that assembly, the Chief Minister announced that the police and the military has been restrained to take any action against the people in the procession. This information was wrongly interpreted by the mob mentality of the crowd as an open invitation to commit violence against the Hindus. The mob mentality was copied by the rival communities easily. So, Hindus looted Muslim shops while Muslims looted Hindus. The police remained immobilized while the mayhem continued unstopped.

Thirteen days ago, Sova's landlord Mr. Sukumar Bhattacharya's eighty- eight years old father had passed away. For the last rites which are conducted on the 13th day after the death of a person, known as ('Shraddh'), Sukumar's five brothers with their families had come to take part in the rituals. They all were tonsured, wearing white clothes, and all five brothers were busy chanting the mantras. The rituals were being held in the open central courtyard of their huge house; the main door was locked for safety. Sukumar's father had built the house and they had been living there for more than 40 years. The neighbors were mostly Muslims, but Sukumar and his brothers had grown up with most of the boys in their neighborhood and knew each of the families across the lane very well. Sukumar was well-loved and respected by his neighbors as he was a gentle soul. His brothers had moved to their own houses and the ancestral house was under Sukumar's care. He diligently distributed the rent earned each month to his brothers' post office account. So, all of them had a very peaceful, loving relationship among themselves.

As the rituals were being performed, Sukumar and his brothers could hear a crowd gathering outside the house. There was a buzzing noise coming from the crowd. As many people were speaking in a hushed tone. Sukumar motioned the priest to lower his voice while chanting the mantras, he didn't want to catch unwanted attention to his house that day.

Sova from her second-floor verandah could see the courtyard where the rituals were being performed and the main door clearly, she had heard the crowd outside the main door. The other tenants had all moved to the verandah, fear on every face. They all knew theirs was a Muslim neighborhood. There were only 3 Hindu houses in the lane. Sova was agitated, she could feel the atmosphere of fear in and around her. She slowly moved back into the room; her baby was napping peacefully. She took her baby and went into the small room at the back of the kitchen. The room was quite dark and big enough for one person, it was used to store coals, wood, etc. She pulled out a wicker basket and placed the baby's bedding inside the basket with her baby in it. Then with a dirty cloth, she hung the basket in the corner of the room on a hook, so the basket kept swinging as the baby moved. It looked like a dirty wicker basket hanging in a dingy room. During lunchtime she had ground poppy seeds and made poppy paste, she had added a bit of the paste to the mashed baby rice while feeding Khuku. She knew with a bit of poppy paste, her baby would sleep peacefully, longer than a child does generally.

By afternoon the news of the communal riot between the Hindus and Muslims had spread like wildfire. The Muslims were entering Hindu houses and slaying the Hindus in Muslim-majority areas. In many Hindu-majority areas, similar incidents were happening to Muslims, where Hindus were attacking the Muslims. The mobs were cloning each other's violent actions. Sova prayed for Nalin's safety and slowly opened her jewelry box. In a jute bag she collected all her gold ornaments, on her finger she wore her most precious ring, her diamond ring. It was gifted by Nalin to her on her wedding night. "It's my mother's", he had said with great love as he had eased the ring into her finger.

Sova unmindfully wore the ring and turned the stone part back into her palms. She didn't know what she was doing but she felt a need to do it.

Suddenly there was a huge knock on the front door. All held their breath. The landlord Sukumar Bhattacharya and his five brothers had all risen from their seating position and were silently standing and looking at the door. The crowd started shouting "Open the door .... you Kafirs…open the door" The women and children of the Bhattacharyas rushed inside their rooms and bolted the doors. Sukumar Da looked up at his tenants and motioned them to enter their rooms and lock up. Sova was standing behind the pillar and watching the scene below. Suddenly there was a huge shout and the crowd was trying to break the main door. The main door was made of very thick wood difficult to break open it was supported by 18 inches of brick walls. It held like a fortress. After trying to push the door open for some time, the mob outside started throwing stones, glass bottles, and wood pieces chanting Allah's name and threatening to kill all the Hindu men. Sova could feel her blood freeze in her veins.

Suddenly they heard a single man's voice from outside "Sukumar…. Suku… It is Karim Chacha speaking. Open the door, we want to talk to you. Don't be frightened your friends Suleman, Iftar, and Abdul are all here. Come out hear us out", the voice was weak and earnest and convincing. Sukumar Da, the landlord looked at his brothers, they held his hand and were shaking their heads warning him not to open the door. The priest was hiding behind the water tank, shivering with fear. There was an eerie silence when another voice boomed "Sukumar, open the door, we want to speak to you…I am Abdul" Sukumar Bhattacharya spoke in a steady voice, "We are performing the last rites of my father". Suddenly hell broke loose…there was a huge commotion outside and suddenly the front door burst open as the unruly mob broke down the door and rushed inside screaming murder. Sova forgot to breathe as she saw the mob lynching the tonsured Bhattacharya brothers, one by one. The first to get a blow on his head was the gentle-natured Sukumar Bhattacharya…someone then cut his throat, and blood spurted out like a fountain from his neck as he fell down clutching his throat… Sova was numb…as the Bhattacharya brothers were being slain one by one, the mass murder continued…the priest was dragged from behind the water tank and fell instantly dead as someone hit his head with a brick. The mayhem continued on the ground floor until all men of the family lay dead. The women of the family stood inside the room, shocked to speak. The children had lost their voices. Shanti was watching the mayhem through the narrow slit of the window. Suddenly the mob started banging on her door and in reflex, Shanti screamed in a strong voice 'No more men are alive in this house, please go" Soon the blood-thirsty mob started climbing the first-floor stairs….

"All men of the house come down we will not hurt the women or children.... only the men come down" someone from the mob cried out. There was no sound. The first-floor tenant Pran Nath was at home but he was hiding inside the water drum. As the mob reached their room, they broke the door, and seeing the fourteen-year-old son Dileep, they pulled him out on the verandah and stabbed him screaming "Allah O Akbar". The father Pran Nath jumped out of the drum screaming in anguish... "Kill me leave him, he is a child...." Before he could complete the sentence, an iron rod had pierced his stomach. The other tenant Pratima stood in a stupor as the men entered her room and ransacked all her belongings, finding no men they left. As the mob left, Ahmed, the neighbor goon stayed back closed the door, and raped her mercilessly...Pratima was still in a stupor, unable to react. Ahmed had been lusting over Pratima for a long time, and that day he got the opportunity.

By the time the mob reached the second floor, they broke into Sova's room, ransacked the room and on the shelf, they found the gold ornaments kept in a jute bag. The mob screamed with joy. "We got gold...we got gold...." Someone did enter the small dark room behind the kitchen used for keeping coal and wood for the stove but finding nothing came out after a while saying "Keo nei...no one's here" gesturing with his hand that no one was there. The mob was satisfied with the loot and moved to the next tenant's room. He was a student, they ransacked his room but he was nowhere to be found. "Come let's go we are done here..." one of the mobsters said loudly. Soon others followed him out, taking anything valuable they could lay their hands on. The sound on the staircase slowly receded…there was an eerie silence …as if all were dead. The stench of death, gore, and blood was slowly rising. From the extended parapet of the terrace, Nitin slowly crept inside his room, he had been hanging on the ledge to save his life. His heart was pounding loudly…he slowly went out of his room and the first thought he had was of Sova and her child. Sova was like an elder sister to him. He entered Sova's room, looking around in apprehension. He slowly walked towards the small room near the kitchen, he could hear the whimpering of the child, as his eyes adjusted in the dark, he saw a deadly sight …amidst the heap of coal was half-hidden Sova…her eyes burning bright with fear of an animal about to ambush.

"Boudi…!!" Nitin called out. Slowly Sova emerged unrecognizable, she had hidden herself in the heap of coal, smearing coal dust all over her body. As they emerged from the dingy room into the ransacked room, Nitin bought Khuku out of her hiding place in the basket. Sova was unaware of what was happening…she remembered the face …the face of Rehman the betel leaf vendor from whom she always bought the betel leaves. He had come inside the small room and as he had kicked the coal heap, he had seen a woman hidden inside, as Sova's eyes met his there was a plea …a fear …he was about to call others …when Sova had joined her hand and had held her diamond ring to him…the sparkle of the ring had made him decide in the speck of a second not to reveal her secret hiding place, deep within he knew if she was found she would be brutally raped by his fellow mobsters. He quickly put the ring on his small finger and said loudly "Keo nei…No one's here" and ran out of the small room.

Nitin made Sova sit on the floor, placed her still-sleeping baby beside her, and slowly tiptoed to check on the rest of the tenants. As he slowly descended the stairs, he could hear footsteps running down from the first floor, his heart missed a beat as his mind questioned "Are they returning?", but the receding footsteps confirmed that whoever the person was, was leaving in a hurry. As he checked Pratima's room, he felt faint, Pratima was lying in a strange position as if a rag doll has been tossed away, her saree and clothes torn, she was bleeding from everywhere… her eyes were open and seemed lifeless…Nitin knew he must call for help, and inform the police but he first wanted to check on the others. On the verandah behind the flowerpots were the dead bodies of Pran Nath and his son Dileep, the mother was inside the house unconscious or dead…Nitin didn't check further, he went to the ground floor and staggered to his core at the scene. All tonsured Brahmin men of the Bhattacharya family were dead on the ground, their white dhotis had turned red soaked in their own blood. Behind the water tank was the priest lying dead. Nitin knocked softly at the closed door, hoping to find the landlady and the rest of her relatives. The landlady Shanti Di was in shock but at the same time, she felt very calm and in control. She said "We must inform the police" Nitin looked at her in fear, "They are still around, I escaped by hiding, they have killed Pran Da and his son too. Pratima di seemed dead. Sova Di and the baby are alive but she is in shock. How do I go out to inform the police?" The landlady took him to the back door of the house and said "Run through this lane, no one comes here as it is used for throwing garbage. As you reach the main road you will be safe. Go to Chief Inspector Sengupta, and tell him Sukumar Bhattacharya's house has been attacked. He will help you."

Four hours later, a big police truck with policemen and women came to the Bhattacharya house, followed by Chief Inspector Sengupta and a few other officers. As they entered the house the gory sight that welcomed them was beyond their imagination. Nitin guided them upstairs where he found Sova still sitting staring into nothingness, smeared in coal dust, her baby was crying. The lady police supported her and took her to the police truck downstairs, Sova was in shock, she could not even hear her baby crying. Another lady police lifted the baby and followed them down. Nitin took the Policemen to Pratima's room, a policeman checked for her pulse, she had a pulse, and she was taken in an ambulance to the hospital. The rest of the women were slowly taken to the police truck. No one was speaking, crying, or saying a word, not even the policemen dared to open their mouths. The sight was so gory no one was sure they could speak a word. The Police truck took all the women to the main Police station for safety.

Chapter **5**

The Aftermath

On the first day of the riot which had started by midmorning and by the time the police could take any action, it was late evening when curfew was imposed in the city of Calcutta. By 9 pm the army troops were deployed in sensitive areas. Irrespective of the military presence the riots continued for the next four days. The first two days of the riots the Muslims had attacked the Hindus with brutality and the Hindus had not put-up resistance as was predicted by the Chief Minister, who had told in his rally that Hindus were frightened of Muslims and would not put up a fight. India had a history of being looted, and plundered by the Mughals invaders and Hindus hardly resisted. But on the third day of the riot, on 18th Aug, a brave Hindu youth named Gopal Mukherjee, a supporter of Netaji Subhas Chandra Bose had gathered Hindu youths and organized an army to take up the Muslim attackers. On the 18th of August morning when the Muslim attackers received resistance from the Hindus, they were surprised. The Muslim goons who were carrying out the mayhem were hunted down by the Hindu youth and met their deserved fate. Had it not been for Gopal Mukherjee, all Hindus would have had to flee from Calcutta, and it would have resulted in the mass exodus of the Hindu community from Bengal.

On 21st August, Bengal was put under Viceroy's rule. Thousands of people had started fleeing from the city to escape death and the city was in mayhem. The British and the Congress party blamed Jinnah for the situation. But supporters of the Muslim League blamed the Congress party for fanning the riots. Thus, the blame game continued while thousands of innocent families lost their loved ones, someone's son…someone's husband, brothers, fathers, and uncles…. some families were left with badly raped, mutilated female members or orphan children ….

The police had set up camps for the victims of the riots, more than 10,000 people were declared dead and 15,000 wounded. The savage manner in which the bodies were mutilated and the savagery of rape victims bore evidence of the communal discord and fundamentalism of the perpetrators. The camps were set up to register the victims, the ones who were injured were sent to hospitals, and the ones who had lost their relatives were asked to give forwarding addresses so their relatives could be informed. As The Bhattacharyas along with Sova and Nitin were the first ones to arrive at the camp, they were called to register their details. Four days had passed but Sova was still in a state of shock, she was sitting staring into nothingness, she did not even react to her crying baby Nitin and the landlady took care of Sova's baby, Shanti Di knew she had to stand strong at such times, she could not let her grief overtake her sense of responsibility towards her co-sisters, their children and her tenants, among whom Sova was in such a state. Pratima, the other tenant who was brutally raped, was fighting for her life in the hospital. Shanti had the support of Nitin, who stood by her like a son in this crisis.

The Police were registering the victims. When they came to Sova, she couldn't speak a word. The Camp doctor was called to assess her condition. The doctor told "She is in shock so her memory has lapsed. She might recover slowly. Where is her husband?"- Nitin looked at Shanti Di, who looked back blankly. In all this chaos they had completely forgotten about Nalin Ghosh, Sova's husband. "He had gone to work that morning but never saw him return"- the landlady said in a low voice, she didn't want Sova to hear her. Sova suddenly started shaking uncontrollably, her limbs stiffened and she lost consciousness and fell on the floor in a heap.

When Sova opened her eyes, she was in the hospital bed. Doctors had told Nitin and Mrs. Bhattacharya that Sova has developed seizures due to extreme stress and she needs time to recover. While Sova was in the hospital, Shanti Di informed the police about Sova's father-in-law's name and position. Hearing that Sova was the daughter-in-law of Rai Saheb Lalit Kanti Ghosh, Chief Inspector Sengupta telephoned Rai Saheb and informed him about his daughter-in-law and his granddaughter. He had also informed him that his son was missing and once Sova is discharged from the hospital, he would personally bring her back home. The only thing Sengupta didn't gauge was the tightness of Rai Saheb's voice and his angry release of breath when he heard the news. Rai Saheb was fuming ... the brunt of his anger was faced by his staff and servants in Delhi, where he was on his 6-month stint. Her destiny was decided way before Sova returned to the house, where she never ever wanted to return.

Chapter 6

The Return Home

It was a dreadful day, it was raining incessantly, 30th of August 1946. The monsoon had set in, the roads were clogged with murky water, and people were rushing around with umbrellas as it had been raining continuously for the past two days. The police jeep was honking and making its way through the crowded street. Chief Inspector Sengupta was cursing under his breath as he was maneuvering the vehicle amidst heavy traffic. Sova was seated in the back seat, holding Khuku tightly. She was just discharged from the hospital, she was given a handful of medicines and told not to get stressed at home, only then she would recover faster. It was the effect of the medicines maybe, Sova was not aware of her feelings. She knew she was returning back to her father-in-law's hell house but she seemed calm, calm in a strange way.

As the jeep entered the gates of the huge house, the servants came rushing to help Sova and the baby get inside the house. Sova was expecting to be thrown out of the house but she could not see her father-in-law around. Mira, Nalin's aunt came and embraced Sova saying "Poor girl look at you, what bad luck.", she didn't say anything further as she ushered Sova to her room. Chief Inspector Sengupta had expected to be thanked by Rai Saheb but seeing him nowhere in sight he left dejected. His chance of being favored by Rai Saheb was lost. Sova looked at her room, where she had arrived as a new bride a few years ago, she remembered how happy both she and Nalin were when they were leaving to set up their own house and now within a year, she was back to the hell hole. She knew what was coming her way....it was just testing her strength...her bad luck....to see how much more can she endure....!

Diary entry: 5th September 1946, 11:30 am

Khuku is playing with the servants. Nalin ...where are you? Why haven't you returned...Almost 20 days are gone by...Come back ...please...!

From the other relatives, Sova came to know that Rai Saheb had informed the Police Superintendent to look for Nalin. He had made it clear that he had no feelings for a son who had chosen to abandon him and his family not even a year ago. For him, such a son was already dead. When Sova came to know this, she knew she needed to do something, she couldn't sit and wait for Nalin to reappear. She needed to know if he was injured in some hospital or at worst killed…. she needed answers …until then she would not be at peace. Deep within she knew Nalin was alive…. he had promised he would be safe…he knew she was all by herself…he must be somewhere injured …. badly injured in some hospital…waiting to be found.

17th September 1946, 10 am

Today my Khuku has turned 1. It is true they say children born in September, the month of the Monsoon have to cry their entire life, they have a sad life. I hope this prediction is false. May my baby reunite with her father. I take a pledge today to gift my daughter her lost father, this will be my gift for her.

Diary entry: 20th September 1946 10:30 pm

Tomorrow I will go to Bow Bazaar, I will go to collect a few of our belongings from that dreadful house. I need to see if Nalin has returned there or not. If any of the neighbors had seen him around. I have asked Aruna Aunty to look after my Khuku while I go there. I hope I get some news about Nalin.

The next morning Sova mustered up all courage to catch a rickshaw and travel to her rented house in Bow bazaar. The streets had police patrolling and the curfew was lifted from 10 am to 6 pm in the evening. Sova pulled the rickshaw hood, she didn't want her father-in-law's acquaintances to inform him that they had seen Sova traveling alone in a rickshaw. Sova urged the Rickshaw puller to run fast as she was feeling very vulnerable traveling alone, all by herself which she had never done. As a lady of a respectable house, she should have been escorted by the family servant or should have used her father-in-law's car. But she did not want to face him yet. She could sense a doom waiting for her in the future. Sova shook her head to shed off all bad thoughts, today she promised herself to remain positive in her thoughts. She had already decided that she will take the course of her life into her own hands. She will find Nalin and she was determined that no one could stop her, not even her father-in-law.

As the rickshaw entered the lanes of Bow Bazar, Sova felt breathless, her heart was pounding loudly, her mouth was dry, and she felt faint. But her inner voice was telling her "You have to face this…for yourself, your daughter, and husband. You need to find Nalin"

As the rickshaw stopped in front of the Bhattacharya's house, the evidence of destruction was evident. The huge strong entrance door was broken, hanging on to its hinges. The iron door handles were dangling and making a soft thudding sound each time the door moved. Sova asked the rickshaw puller to rest as she would take some time to gather her belongings. She went inside the courtyard, the same courtyard which was strewn with corpses, blood, and gore a few weeks ago. Someone had cleaned the blood stains but the images of death were so strong in her mind that Sova could clearly see the bodies even if there were none. Seeing her entering the landlady came out hurriedly "Sova…. Sova…how are you dear?" her voice was unsteady. Sova hugged her and both of them started weeping. Later as she sat in her room, Nitin came down. He was relieved to find that Sova was fine. Nitin said that he had enquired in the neighborhood shops, but no one had seen Nalin return when the riot had started. "Pratima di is still in hospital", Nitin said sadly, "her brothers have come, as soon as she is discharged from the hospital, they will take her back to their village. She doesn't recognize anyone; she screams in fear if anyone comes near her. She has lost her mental balance after the horrific rape she was subjected to."

Sova could not stop the stream of tears flowing down her cheeks.

"Nitin, will you help me brother", Sova looked at Nitin.

" Yes Didi, I am like your brother, please tell me how can I help", Nitin spoke earnestly.

"Nitin, I have decided to go to Nalin's Post Office and ask the Post Master about him. He was supposed to keep his employees safe. He must know the whereabouts of Nalin", Sova said.

Nitin said, "Yes let's go. I am sure we will get some information from there".

Sova knew her father-in-law had filed a missing people's report for his son in the Police station but with thousands of people missing, dead, or injured, it would take a long time for the police to come up with results. Sova was not ready to wait any longer. She had made up her mind.

Sova then went to her room upstairs, entering the room she didn't have the courage to collect anything from there. She went to the rack where she kept the small brass idol of Lord Krishna she lovingly called "Bal Gopal" given to her by her mother. The idol had fallen to the side but was safe. She took her Bal Gopal and tiptoed out of the room. She knew she could never forget the mayhem she had witnessed in that house, years later she would dream of the room and the fear would always return and she would have seizures.

Sova bid goodbye to her landlady, and told her she would come to meet her in case ever Nalin showed up there. Sova told the rickshaw puller to take them to the Bow Bazaar Post office. The post office was located on Bow Bazaar's main road and was part of a grand old building. As they entered the Post office, they could see all the officials were busy with their work. Nitin guided Sova to the Post master's office. In a cabin was seated a typical Bengali babu, with square framed glasses and a protruding belly. He was busy with his paperwork.

"Mr. Mukherjee", Nitin called for his attention. Mr. Mukherjee lifted his face, he had thick black eyebrows and looked very annoyed at being disturbed. "Sir, this is Mrs. Sova Ghosh, your employee Mr. Nalin Ghosh's wife. She has come with some queries." Nitin spoke. Mr. Mukherjee looked at Sova, who looked pale and troubled. He gestured for them to enter his room, "Please sit-down Mrs. Ghosh, how can I help you?"

Sova frowned and asked, "Sir, where is Nalin?" There was a minute's silence which was like an eternity to Sova, Mukherjee spoke up equally surprised "Well Nalin left for home on the 16th of August afternoon, the moment he heard your area was being attacked by the Muslim mob.

We told him not to go but he was adamant saying his wife and child are alone and he needed to be with them"

No one said a word for some time, by this time other office employees had all hurdled in the Postmaster's room. Someone from the back asked, "Did Nalin not return home?" The eeriness of the question haunted everyone. Sova could not even shake her head to say 'No'.

One of his colleagues said, "Nalin Da had told me that he would take some shortcut route to his house, from some lane which was used for dumping the garbage, no one used it so he would be safe if he went from there."

Nitin exclaimed, "Yes, I know that garbage dump lane, I had used it to come to the Police station after the rioters had left. My landlady had told me about it."

Mr. Mukherjee shook his head and said, "Where did he go then?" No one dared even guess or speculate as Sova swooned and fell back on her chair. There was a commotion as everyone started to make an effort to bring young Sova back to her senses. Someone sprinkled water on her face, Sova gained her senses and sat with a perturbed look on her face. Her young face had paled and she looked disoriented. Slowly regaining composure, she rose from her chair and told Nitin "Let's go". Mr. Mukherjee said in a sad voice "Sorry Mrs. Ghosh, I will send my people to check the hospitals to see if Nalin had been admitted to any of them". Sova could feel hot tears forming behind her eyes. She joined her hands to say thanks to the Postmaster and left his office. Her hope of getting any news of Nalin was a distant reality now but she heard her inner voice say "I will find him no matter what".

As Nitin and Sova sat in the rickshaw, Sova told Nitin "Nitin, from tomorrow I will go to each hospital in this area and check for Nalin. What if he is lying in one of the hospitals and none of us have bothered to find him? Nitin are you with me, will you come with me?"

Nitin put his hands on Sova's hands reassuringly "Didi, of course, we will search for Nalin Da and find him" Sova dropped Nitin at the lane leading to his house and asked the rickshaw puller to take her back to Shyam Bazar, to her father-in-law's house.

It became a routine thereafter, every morning at 10 am Sova would drop her baby at Aruna auntie's and would take the rickshaw to Bow Bazar, pick up Nitin and both of them would go to hospitals in the Bow Bazar area. They would check the patient list, check the wards, bed by bed, and patient by patient to see whether Nalin was admitted to the hospital or not. They also checked the morgue, and the list of unclaimed dead bodies to double-check that they are not missing any lead. By 5:30 pm Sova would return home, her thin face tired with the disappointment at not finding her husband. She was obsessed with one task, the task of finding her husband. The old maid Dhanoi had asked her a few times "Where are you going every day?". But Sova had not answered because she knew if she spoke, she would be blamed for all the misfortunes. Sova couldn't deal with that now, she had a mission to fulfill, a mission to find her lost husband.

Sova and Nitin made a list of all hospitals in North Calcutta and each day tried covering at least one hospital to check it thoroughly to find Nalin. They even went to mental hospitals, makeshift camps where riot victims were stationed and kept searching. Then started broadening their area of search from north Calcutta to east, west, and south. Months passed. But the determination of Sova did not waver, her life's aim was to search for Nalin.

Chapter 7
The Remedy for Torment

Months passed. On 1st January 1947. Sova had gone out at 10 am and by the time she returned home, it was almost 6 pm. The curfew has been lifted from the city. As she opened the main gate and walked inside the house, she felt uncomfortable, she looked up, and to her horror, she saw her father-in-law standing right in front of her on the verandah looking at her, she could feel his hatred transmitting through the air towards her. His six months work stint at Delhi was over, now he would stay in Calcutta for the next 6 months.

"Stop there", Rai Saheb roared at Sova. Sova stood still. She felt faint but stood still. "Where had you been?"-Rai Saheb asked in contempt. Sova couldn't speak, she would rather not speak. There was an uncomfortable silence. Dhanoi spoke loudly," Dada babu, every day she goes out at 10 am and returns by 6 pm. God knows where she goes every day, she tells no one. What a curse to this family, this 'Ghoda Bou'".

Sova was quite tall for her age when she married Nalin, she continued growing taller and very soon she was taller than Nalin. Behind their back, Dhanoi had started calling her 'Ghoda Bou' meaning Horse Bride. Sova stood there her brain trying not to register the insults and the accusations, which she knew she was destined to hear.

Dhanoi was full of venom, she decided to spit it out at that very moment. She knew Rai Saheb was very angry and it was the perfect day to use the venom she had harbored in her heart against Sova effectively.

"Look at her Dada babu, look…her husband is missing for so many months but look at her, her beauty has not diminished. She's glowing like a moon. She goes for outings, God knows with whom…No one questions her, she is living her life."

Rai Saheb cursed in a thunderous voice "Kulochini Kulnashak" (it means destroyer of one's own family). You witch you killed my son; it was because of you he had left this house and went to stay in a rented house. You are his killer. You have destroyed my family, you are the reason why my son is missing or maybe dead…. you are a witch. I will burn you to death."

Before his horrid words would end, Sova started shaking violently, her limbs got stiffened, and her jaw got jammed as she suffered a major epileptic seizure, which always got aggravated in stressful situations. She fell on the floor in a heap. Rai Saheb thundered a few more curses and walked back to his room. The servants hurriedly picked Sova and took her to her room.

This became a regular occurrence: Rai Saheb would utter the worst of abuses, and Dhanoi would add crude remarks on Sova's enhanced physical beauty which was somehow not diminishing in spite of all her bad fortunes. Sova was just 22 years old, how could she possibly lose all her youth and charm in a few days…. she wanted to look old, and ugly so as to stop the baseless toxicity heaped on her but she was helpless. She was a young beautiful woman, a young mother…. how can she suddenly turn ugly…how will her body know her husband is missing and so she needs to look ugly… These stressful situations and mental and emotional torture resulted in her seizures, almost every day.

The next few weeks Sova was very ill, and the seizures worsened. She was unconscious and on her bed for days together. The family doctor Dr. Sudeep was aware of Sova's mental condition and the reasons for her seizures. He advised complete bed rest to avoid any stressful situation in the future, both Rai Saheb and Dhanoi were disinterested in the doctor's advice.

Seeing the terrible phase in Sova's life, Rai Saheb's younger brother Ronit Kanti decided to leave aside his ego to be at his elder brother's side in times of trouble and try to help Sova in his own way. He came to speak to Rai

Saheb every evening to support him and enquire about his nephew Nalin. Ronit came to know that the Police were still searching for him but there was no trace.

"Hundreds are missing," Raisaheb said bluntly, "if he was dead, we could have found his body but I think he is too ashamed to return to my house, so he is absconding." These last words were filled with deep hatred, Ronit could sense his elder brother's hatred towards his son was deeper than he had gauged. Ronit knew Sova's life would be hell for the next six months as Rai Saheb would ensure he took his grudge out on his unfortunate daughter-in-law.

Ronit went home that night and was lost in deep thought when Aruna came to serve him dinner.

Aruna asked "What's wrong? You look worried?" Ronit sat down to eat, "Yes I am worried about Sova and the child"

Aruna looked at him and said "What happened, Khuku is being taken care of by me. Sova is unable to get up from the bed and I am helping her. I am not complaining"

Aruna had developed a great bond with Sova's daughter Khuku. She always wanted a daughter as she had two sons. She adored Khuku, feeding her, and taking care of her and Khuku too was comfortable with her. For the last few months Sova would leave Khuku with Aruna Aunty without giving a second thought, she knew Ronit uncle and Aruna Aunty were God sent and would keep her daughter safe.

Ronit said gravely, "Dada, will never forgive Sova, never allow her to live in peace if Nalin doesn't return. Even if he returns, he would make their lives hell. I know my brother; he is filled with anger and hatred for those two young people. I pity Sova…. I doubt she will ever recover in this situation."

Aruna knew what her husband was saying was the truth. Sova would never recover if she faces such stress at home. She said, "Why don't you think of something for Sova, something that will keep her busy or engaged? She seemed quite determined to search for Nalin. She was doing good then. She had an aim, an aim to search for her husband. But now …. maybe she needs something to get her going…"

Ronit Kanti agreed and said "Yes, she needs a purpose in life to live. I will see what can be done."

The next morning, on his way to his office, the Indian Press, he went to 'The Nari Sahayata Kendra' a welfare organization set up by the government of Bengal for the welfare and benefit of women who have lost their families and livelihood in the riot. He met the Centre head Mr. Goyal, who showed him where the destitute women stayed in the Kendra, and learned Sewing, stitching, and embroidery. They were given basic education and then were placed in small-scale factories so that they could earn their livelihood and be independent.

"Mr. Goyal", Ronit Kanti said, "our daughter-in-law is in need of a job. She has completed high school, is an excellent cook, she can sew, embroider and stitch. I have seen her handiwork. Can you give her a job in your center? She needs to come out of her depressive state and live life, her husband, my nephew, is missing since the riots."

Ronit narrated Sova's sad story. Mr. Goyal told Ronit Kanti to come with Sova and fill out the form then he could help. Ronit informed him that Sova was unwell and would come once she was better. With one work done, Ronit had a greater task at hand, and that was to convince his brother Rai Saheb to agree to allow Sova to go and work in the Nari Sahayata Kendra. Ronit knew his elder brother would not allow any female from his family to go out to work. It would be an insult to his position. Ronit had a better idea. He took Dr Sudeep, the family doctor into confidence. Dr Sudeep agreed to the suggestion that Sova would recover faster if she stayed less in the stressful surrounding of the house. Also earning her own money would give her confidence and an aim to live her life. So, it was decided that Dr. Sudeep would suggest Rai Saheb of Sova's job at the Nari Sahayata Kendra as a teacher and would assure him that he would not let anyone know that Sova was working. Dr. Sudeep convinced Rai Saheb that it was the only solution to cure Sova, who had almost given up on her will to live. After Dr. Sudeep's week-long persuasive logical reasonings, Rai Saheb grudgingly agreed.

Two months later Sova started going to the Nari Sahayata Kendra to teach sewing, stitching, and embroidery to the women there and as she met women with woes like hers, she started healing bit by bit. Khuku, her baby was being taken care of by Aruna Aunty. In the evening when she returned home Khuku would come to her reluctantly. Sova knew she was being unfair to her baby by not being with her but she knew she had to be strong and earn and save money for their future. She knew her father-in-law was capable of throwing both of them out of his house, at his whim. She wanted to be self-dependent and she knew she had to sacrifice her maternal love for the greater good.

Being an excellent teacher and an empathetic person by nature, Sova was well respected in the Nari Kendra. The women of the Kendra started stitching trousers, and shirts, making bedspreads, and embroidering them beautifully. These items were sold at greater prices and the money earned was used to run the Kendra very well. Within 6 months the Nari Sahayata Kendra earned the most revenue. Soon an eminent minister was due to visit the Kendra to congratulate the women. This particular minister was responsible for the efficient working of this Kendra from the beginning. Sova and the other women started preparing for the Minister's visit and grand welcome. Sova had decided to stitch a Kashmiri Pashmina shawl for the minister. Mr. Goyal was happy that his Nari Kendra was becoming so famous and the star worker was Rai Saheb's daughter-in-law Sova. He respected her a lot.

Chapter 8

JAAN BARI

Nitin came to visit Sova in the Nari Sahayata Kendra once or twice a week. They would go in search of Nalin in different destitute homes or hospitals in and around Calcutta. Nitin was studying and whenever he got free time, he continued the search all by himself. Like a dedicated younger brother, Nitin was with Sova through thick and thin.

One day Nitin came to the Nari Kendra all excited. "Didi, Sova Di"- Nitin called out seeing Sova busy. "I have an interesting thing to tell to you". Sova made him sit in the front office, finished her instructions to the ladies, and came a bit later. "Tell me Nitin, what's so important"- Sova heaved and sat down on the wooden chair.

Nitin spoke excitedly "Have you heard of Jaan Baari?"

Sova looked at him quizzically and shook her head in denial.

Nitin said "Well, I heard from my college friend Raghav, there is a tantric in Jaan Bari, a renowned person, who can predict anyone's present, past and future. He also helps in finding missing persons. Let's go and meet this Tantric." Sova had all ears for what Nitin was saying. "Really is there someone around who can tell something about Nalin?" Sova felt a ray of hope in her otherwise desolate existence. Nitin said "Didi, Raghav stays near that place he told me the history. You know the history of Jaan Bari dates back to the rule of Maharaja Krishna Chandra Roy of Nadia."

Sova was curious but doubtful, "Tantra Shastra, I have heard it is associated with black magic, I wouldn't want to get myself into any more trouble than I already am in." Nitin smiled. "Sova Di, it's a misconception. Tantra Shastra is not black magic. It is a system of invoking spiritual energy." Nitin decided to impart his newly gained knowledge of Tantra Shastra to Sova, his friend Raghav had recently enlightened him on it.

"These spiritual energies are used for spiritual development. Through the rituals, one's past or future can be predicted by the tantric. Genuine tantric do not misuse their knowledge."

Sova found herself drawn to this new idea. Nitin continued "So as I was narrating the history of Jaan Baari. Maharaja Krishna Chandra Roy of Nadia had gifted 200 bighas of land to the most learned Brahmin of his court. This Brahmin priest who was the descendant of a scholar Brahmin Achyut Panchanan, a noted sage, once found the idol of Mother Goddess Kali carved of black stone in the river. He brought the idol home and started worshipping it daily. Later his descendants continued worshipping the Goddess through generations. The descendants of this Brahmin were all highly knowledgeable scholars, all excelling in Astrology, Astronomy, Shastras, and Tantra Shastras. Thus, their house came to be known as 'Gyaan Baari' meaning the house of Knowledge. From the word 'Gyaan' the word 'Jaan' emerged as a simplified version, hence people started calling their house "Jaan Bari"

Nitin was pleased he could impress Sova for once with his knowledge, she sat listening to him with childlike curiosity. Clearing his voice Nitin continued "Srimat Achyut Panchanan was a brilliant astrologer, who could accurately predict the past and the future based on his perfect astrological calculations. Kings, queens, elites, ministers, traders, and the poorest of the poor, the misfortunate ones, everyone thronged his house to know about their future. It's said great people like the great scholar Ishwar Chandra Vidyasagar, spiritual gurus Ramkrishna Thakur and Sharada Ma had visited him."

Sova didn't waste time to decide that she needed to go to Jaan Baari to know about Nalin's whereabouts. The following Saturday, a week later Sova confirmed to Nitin that she would go with him to Jaan Bari. Saturdays were mostly free for Sova, as her students would wind up their handiwork made during the week, and pack them carefully to be shipped to different vendors. In the meantime, Nitin made all arrangements to go to Dalalpukur, where 'Jaan Baari 'was located.

On Saturday early morning, Sova and Nitin took a bus to Dalalpukur, some 10 km away from her home. It took them almost 2 hours to change buses to reach Jaan Baari. As they entered the temple complex, Nitin pointed at the Kali temple and said "The actual Goddess Kali idol found in the river is kept hidden in a chest below the main temple. The sage Panchanan Pandit was a 'Baam-Margi', an orthodox tantric worshipper of Goddess Kali and he practiced tantric rituals. Later his descendants followed the same planetary calculations so their predictions are most accurate. The Brahmin scholar we are going to meet is his 5th generation descendant". Sova nodded, she had carried all relevant information about Nalin's exact day, time, and year of birth, his horoscope made at his birth, in case it was required. She had so many questions to ask the tantric.

After waiting for an hour, they were guided to a smaller chamber of the temple complex. There was an air of eeriness in the chamber, human skulls and bone were strategically placed around a Yajna Kunda, the fire pit, used for religious purposes. It was smeared with red vermilion and sacrificial blood markings. There was smoke emitting from the fire pit and behind the pit was seated a man who looked as if in deep meditation, a white dhoti covered his lower body, while his upper body was covered by necklaces made of bones and weird-looking beads, his face was glowing in the orange flame, a long vermillion mark on his forehead and his hair tied in a bun over his head. His eyes were closed as Sova and Nitin quietly settled down opposite the fire pit on the mat. The room was deafeningly quiet….an uncomfortable silence…both Sova and Nitin were unsure about their next step, were they supposed to speak, or keep quiet, will the Tantric open his eyes and speak to them…or is he meditating. As these thoughts were running through their mind, suddenly the flames started flickering and the crackling sound of the amber-colored burning twigs filled the chamber with strange subdued eeriness.

Sova saw the Tantric open his eyes and looked directly at her. Sova was hypnotized for a few seconds by his luminous eyes when she heard his booming voice "Your husband is not dead. He has lost his memory. He has wandered to some unknown place and does not remember. One day he will return back. Wait for him" With these words the Tantric closed his eyes and with his hand gesture, he dismissed them. Sova couldn't speak or ask anything. She was overwhelmed. As Sova and Nitin came out of the Tantric's chamber, she felt very light, as if a heavy stone has been lifted from her head. She now knew why her husband has not returned to her. He has not absconded as her father-in-law had implicated but has lost his memory. This prediction made Sova breathe a full lung of air, for once, after a long time. She felt hope for herself and her daughter. She knew she had to wait for Nalin to come back to her. Sova returned home with hope in her heart to her small daughter, who was unaware of all the trials and tribulations her mother was going through, she was happy in her own innocent world.

Chapter 9
Nari Sahayata Kendra

Sova had an extra spright on her steps, an extra zest for work and an extra enthusiasm for her future. Whenever she would go out to work, her eyes would scan the streets for a familiar face, a face, she was promised would come back to her, a face that would make her life normal again. Khuku was now almost two years of age. She has been learning poems and songs taught by Aruna Aunty. Sova started taking more care of Khuku than before. At night lying on bed, Sova would talk to Khuku telling her about all that she did during the day and all her efforts to find her father and how life would be fun and joyful if her father returns home. Khuku would fall asleep, unable to understand what her mother was saying to her.

In the meantime, in the Nari Sahayata Kendra, the Minister of Women Welfare's visit was due in two days. All preparations were in full swing. Mr. Goyal had arranged for lunch and the women of the Kendra had volunteered to cook. Sova was responsible for the overall management of the events. On the designated day the Minister Mr. Sukumar Bhakt came with his officials. They were greeted by the women with garlands, and the Pashmina shawl that Sova had embroidered was presented to him. He gave a speech on how he would ensure each woman would be self-dependent and he would look after their needs. He toured the Kendra, to see the dormitories where the women stayed, he went to the workshop where they worked and the dining hall where he was served a sumptuous lunch. It was during lunchtime; some women were given the responsibility of serving the minister and his officials. They all sat along with Mr. Goyal and were having lunch. When Swapna, a young widow was serving the Minister. As Swapna walked toward the Minister to serve him a second helping of rice, she suddenly shrieked and fell unconscious. The Minister looked very annoyed. Sova along with other women carried Swapna away and soon other women took over and started serving the guest efficiently, the rest of the lunch hour ended peacefully. Sova sat with Swapna in the infirmary, which was a small room and Dr Rajat Sen, an octogenarian ran his practice there. After the lunch, the Minister met Mr. Goyal for some time in his office. The infirmary was just next to Mr. Goyal's office and Sova could hear the minister speak rudely to Mr. Goyal. "What the hell, can't you manage a few widowed women? See the way that rascal shrieked seeing me….am I a monster?" Mr. Goyal was speaking in a low voice "Sorry Sir, I will make sure nothing like this happens" "Yes, do that"- the minister spoke gruffly, "…. but the food was good and who was the woman who made the shawl…?" Mr. Goyal murmured, "Sova, her husband is missing."

Sova could feel her ears burning, her brain freezing. She was slowly realizing this world was not so good as it seemed, people do not help for the sake of helping others but there is always some ulterior motive in their act of kindness. Sova understood the reason Swapna had fainted seeing the Minister, there was some ugly sinister thing going on in the Kendra in the name of women's welfare. Sova had never stayed there as a resident so she was not aware of these things. Moreover, she was Rai Saheb's daughter-in-law, which gave her a level of protection from many unpleasant things, and she realized it at that very moment.

After the Minister left, Mr. Goyal called the women to thank them for making the event successful. He did mention that Swapna's incident was the only hitch. All women returned back to their dormitory to rest. Sova stayed back to speak to Mr. Goyal.

Mr. Goyal spoke gratefully "Sova, I want to congratulate you, you worked so hard and made this event successful. I am really grateful to you and the women."

Sova spoke grimly and to the point "Goyal Da, I respect you but I am not a fool I saw and heard things that I do not like. Can you explain why Swapna became unconscious seeing the minister?"

Mr. Goyal looked alarmed but seeing the anger brewing in Sova's eyes he decided to reveal the truth to her. Mr. Goyal knew Sova was well connected and would create a hue and cry if she came to know of the wrong things happening at the Kendra. She might put him in trouble. "Please sit down", Mr. Goyal looked pleadingly at Sova. As Sova sat Mr. Goyal cleared his throat and said grimly, "Sova, this minister is a corrupted man. He is helping this Kendra run with Government aid and all other facilities because he wants something in return. He wants young women to be sent to him every week. His car comes at night and we send one woman every week. If I deny him, he will discredit me and ensure we get no aid from the government, in that case, I cannot run this Kendra and all these women have to leave and face even worst situations. Tell me what should I do?" Sova was surprised to hear that these unfortunate women were being used for the flesh trade and they didn't even raise their voices because they had a shelter and work in the Nari Kendra. They wanted nothing more.

Sova remembered in the beginning when she had come to the Kendra, she had asked whether she could get a place to stay for herself and her daughter in the Nari Kendra, as she did not want to stay at her in-law's house but Mr. Goyal had said "No children are allowed in this Kendra, it was the Welfare Minister's order" Now Sova understood why no children were allowed in this place. Sova could say nothing, as she went home that day, all her troubles have returned to her in double fold. She knew she will not be able to work there much longer as the Minister had noticed her and like her bad luck, he too would not leave her so soon. She needed to have an alternative plan for herself and her baby.

Nitin often visited Sova in the Nari Niketan. Sova told Nitin about the debauchery taking place in the Nari Niketan in the name of women's welfare. Nitin assured Sova that he would speak to his college youth leaders and see how the minister could be exposed. Sova knew, the power of youth. Bengali youth were known for their patriotism, bold demeanor, and progressive thoughts, they would not hesitate to speak up against any kind of injustice. So Sova knew Nitin and his friends would help the poor women suffering in these camps.

A few weeks later, an article was published in the Bengali newspaper regarding the exploitation of women in the Nari Kendras around Calcutta. University students gheraoed the welfare minister, who under pressure had to resign. Sova read the news and kept a tab on the developments and was glad that the women of the Nari Sahayata Kendras' would get some justice and peace. These were the small victories that kept her going.

But Sova's own life was not going to be peaceful at all. She was the Floating leaf, wandering in the wind from one trouble to another…. It was not long before she faced another challenging situation in life.

Diary Entry: 15th August 1947 12:00 am

Today at midnight 12:00 am, our country India has become free from British rule. There is happiness all around. People are bursting crackers and celebrating. Tomorrow morning will be a new beginning for my country. One year has gone by since Nalin had gone missing. I am still waiting for him; people sneer at me as I put vermillion on my forehead. I am not a widow, I still believe Nalin is alive. He will return. I cannot stop hoping for his return. I will cling to his memories till he comes back to me.

Chapter 10

A Strange Request

It was the month of April, the year was 1948, Sova was returning back home from the Nari Sahayata Kendra, Rai Saheb saw her and got extremely angry, he started hurling abuses and called her all sorts of degrading names. Sova felt she could melt and disappear in shame but she stood hearing to the insult because she had no other option. The world outside would devour and destroy her if they could lay a finger on her. For her and her daughter's safety, she needed to stay in this house and bear all insults till her husband comes to rescue her from hell.

Sova was no longer the naïve girl who had come to Calcutta as a teenage bride. Back then she had only bookish knowledge but in the last 8 years, life had taught her so much more. She learned how to identify people, all that seems good was not always good. She knew she had to use her knowledge, her intuition, and the sixth sense that every woman possesses to find out a way for herself and her daughter.

A week later on Sunday Sova was at home. On Sundays, she took care of Khuku. She had bathed her and was feeding her, it was 11:30 am in the morning when Aruna Aunty and Ronit Uncle came to her room. Sova cleared the clothes lying on the bed, tidied the chairs, and offered them to sit, while she finished feeding her toddler. Khuku gave a squeal of delight seeing Aruna Aunty. She squirmed off from Sova's arms and ran to Aruna Aunty, who beamed with love and happiness, seeing the toddler preferring her to Sova. Sova noticed this and there was a pang in her heart, she sensed something bad was about to happen.

Ronit Uncle cleared his throat and looking straight at Sova said "Sova, your father-in-law had asked me to convey to you that henceforth you cannot stay here in his house. He does not want to be reminded of his bad luck, which he does every time he sees you."

The brutal words of Ronit uncle came as arrows and went deep into Sova's heart but she felt nothing, she knew her father-in-law hated her. "I have argued with him and he is adamant that you cannot stay in this house. But he has agreed to get you settled in Boral, our ancestral village on the outskirts of Calcutta. We have a village house there, you can go and stay there, he will send you an allowance every month. Our cousin brother Brata's widow also stays there with her daughters, she will help you settle there." Sova was astounded by this news.

Both Ronit uncle and Aruna were looking uncomfortably at Sova, who seemed to be lost in a deep frown. Ronit uncle clearing his throat spoke somberly "I know you must be thinking of your baby's future. Correct, her future will be doomed. There is no school in the village, she will not get any education there" Ronit Uncle had prepared his speech and knew when to lay stress on her helpless situation. There was a pause, Sova felt her mind go blank for a second. But then she felt a strange calmness come over her. Sova had learned through her experience that when someone is so eager to help, it meant they want something from you. But what she was not prepared for was what these two sympathetic people wanted from her. She waited for them to reveal.

By this time Khuku had fallen asleep on Aruna Aunt's lap, Sova went to take Khuku from Aruna Aunty but Khuku was holding her saree tightly, and was unwilling to let go, even in her sleep.

"See, how attached she is with Aruna", Ronit uncle pointed to Sova.

"I want to suggest something, for the future of your daughter, we are ready to adopt her." There was a pause…a deadly silence when Sova could hear the clock ticking steadily, reminding her how helpless she was in her situation. "I have two sons, she will be our only daughter, we will educate her, get her married when she grows up, and all her responsibility will be ours. You on the other hand can be free to either go back to your parents, get remarried, or wait for Nalin in Boral village. It's your life after all" Ronit Kanti finished his prepared speech with a breath. He had been practicing this speech because he was nervous, nervous because his wife would not bear the separation from Khuku, and he was nervous because he could never have another child of his own. Diabetes had turned him impotent.

The impact of Ronit uncle's words was so great that Sova staggered mentally. She took some minutes to understand his proposal. Ronit Uncle and Aruna aunt wanted to adopt her Khuku and give her a stable life, so she would be free to choose her life. "Is this what they meant?" Sova was asking this question to herself. Seeing her confused and dazed, Aruna Aunty quipped in, "Sova, take your time, think over what is good for your daughter, then decide. You have always trusted me with your baby and I have taken care of her as a mother. Now as a mother, you have to think about the welfare of your daughter"

It was an awkward situation, no one knew what else to say. Sova was dumbstruck and lost in thought. Ronit and his wife were unsure of their next step so they left Sova's room, placing Khuku in the baby cot. While Sova sat looking at the empty chairs, her mind was completely blank. She had no strength to think straight.

That night as Sova lay down on her bed, her eyes had a faraway look. She remembered her last few days in her rented house in Bow Bazaar after Khuku was born. Nalin had come from his office and was cradling the baby, cooing and making baby noises as if speaking to her. Sova had brought the evening tea for him, as they sat to drink the tea Nalin had said "I will name my daughter 'Lily', she is the white Lily. Sova laughed and said" "You are keeping an English name for our daughter, especially now when we are at last inching towards freedom, her name will not be appreciated at all in free India''. Nalin smiled and nodded and said "I want to name her after my father "Lalit". Now it was Sova's turn to frown, and she asked, "WHY?" Nalin smiled a sad smile and said "My father hates me, but I do admire his zest for education, he holds such a high post in the Government, all because he is highly educated. I want my daughter to be as educated as him. I want to make my daughter his equivalent so he never looks down upon me. I want to educate my daughter" Sova realized how much Nalin wanted to be loved and respected by his father because whatever he had done in life, was never enough for his father. He was the Rai Saheb, his son was an ordinary Post office employee. Had Rai Saheb given his son a chance, had Nalin not got lost in the riot, had he been there, he too would have reached the post of Chief Post Master, with age and experience but he didn't get a chance …did he?

Sova knew in her husband's absence she had to fulfill her husband's dream of getting their daughter good education…. she was ready to live that dream, to fulfill it would be her dream thence. Now she had two reasons to live. One, to find Nalin, and second to fulfill his dream. Sova decided to name her baby Lily as was her husband's wish, even though she was not very convinced about the name herself.

Chapter **11**

Boral Gram: The Ancestral Village

After hearing from Ronit uncle about her father-in-law's plan to send her to Boral village. Sova remembered her first visit to the village, just after she had got married, some 8 years back. Rai Saheb was posted in Delhi, then. One day Nalin had come from his work and had asked Sova to pack a suitcase, the next day they would travel to their ancestral village - Boral.

The journey by bus was quite tiring as the overcrowded bus was running on dusty roads filled with potholes and the passengers were getting tossed around in the bumpy ride. Sova had managed to get a seat. Boral was situated on the outskirts of Calcutta. They reached their destination and got down from the bus on the highway, there was a rusted tin board pointing towards a kutcha road that led to the village. The road was muddy and uneven, Nalin and Sova continued walking for a while when they could see the village pond lined by coconut and palm trees, they had walked about two kilometers to reach the village. The village was not planned, there were clusters of huts built haphazardly. Dirty water was flowing down the kutcha road creating muddy puddles. The huts had thatched roofs made of straw and palm leaves, and most of the houses were made of mud and straw. Only a handful of houses were made of baked bricks. As they continued walking a few people recognized Nalin and greeted him. By this time the village children had gathered around Nalin and Sova and were looking at Sova in utter amazement, walking along with them in excitement. Sova smiled at the children. The village Headman peeped out of his house, which looked well-built with bricks and proper clay tiles. Nalin stopped to introduce him to Sova, after promising to bring her to his house later, Nalin took Sova to his ancestral house, which was no better than most of the houses in the village. As Sova entered a haggard-looking woman in a tattered saree emerged. Nalin exclaimed "Rita Kaki (Aunt)!" he stooped down to touch her feet in respect. Sova did the same. "So, this is your bride, I am happy you remember me and have come here", Rita Kaki was the widowed wife of Rai Saheb's cousin brother Brata. "Come in, come in", she invited both of them inside the house. The room was empty, a cot was placed in the room where Sova and Nalin sat, while Rita Kaki went to fetch water for them.

Nalin had told Sova on their journey that Rita Kaki was Brata uncle's widow and stayed in the village house with her two teenage daughters. Rai Saheb sent some allowance for them every month. Sova saw two young girls peeping from behind the door. She called them inside, they entered shyly, both were wearing tattered clothes. Nalin had brought sarees and clothes for them which Sova handed to them. There was a spark of happiness in the girls otherwise dry sad face. Nalin introduced them, while they touched their feet, paying their respect. "This is Sonali and this is Rupali, my cousin sisters."

Sova asked them "How are you both?", the girls said something inaudibly. They were just a few years younger than Sova but were ill-nourished and looked very pale. Sova went inside to see what Rita Kaki (Aunt) was doing in the kitchen. There she saw Rita Kaki sobbing and drying her eyes simultaneously. Sova went and sat beside her, for a few minutes they both sat without speaking. Sova held Rita Kaki's hands and asked her what was the matter. Rita Kaki wiped her eyes and said "You are the new bride, you have come to meet me and look at me, unlucky me, I have nothing to offer to you. No food, no gift …. nothing" She continued crying softly. Sova said "Don't worry Kaki, I have come to meet you…I am just like your daughter." Rita Kaki touched Sova's hand in appreciation, Sova could feel her dried hard palms dig into her skin. Kaki pointed at the utensils and said "Nothing is there …no grains….no vegetables…What will I cook …What will I feed you…?" Looking around the kitchen Sova realized the poverty they were living in. There were hardly any grains, rice, or vegetables. Only a few empty utensils were on the shelf.

Sova went and informed Nalin discreetly about the pathetic condition of his auntie's kitchen. Nalin had a deep thoughtful frown on his forehead as he headed to the village market to buy vegetables, groceries, and fish, to be cooked for lunch. When he returned, Sova and the girls got busy cooking lunch. Nalin noticed the house was not in good shape from the inside. The roof was destroyed by years of neglect and his relatives were literally living in abject poverty, which was so evident. Nalin felt ashamed at the misery in which one of his relatives lived. Nalin knew his father was supposed to send allowance to Kaki every month, but was he not sending her the money? This question troubled him, he thought of asking his aunt about this later.

After lunch, they rested for a while, and by evening Nalin and Sova went to the village temple for the evening prayers and Nalin showed her their rice fields and stretch of their farming land. The village headman was walking along with them. "Where is the village school?" Sova asked the headman. He looked a bit unnerved and said hesitatingly "Actually Rai Saheb said next summer he will build a school for us in this village, as of now we have no school in this village. Some children travel to the neighboring village which has a school." Sova was surprised to know that the village had no school which meant most of the children were not getting any education. She thought of Kaki's daughters, they too had no access to education.

The next day Nalin went to meet the headman and the farmers of his fields to check on the crops being sowed that season. Sova was helping Kaki to cook lunch. Rita Kaki sighed and said "My life is hell here Sova, your father-in-law sends money to the village headman who gives me just half of the amount and keeps the rest. If I protest, he threatens to tell everyone that I am a prostitute and should be thrown out of this village. Rai Saheb trusts him and he too will not support me. So, I keep mum and suffer. I go to the field and work hard to earn a few extra coins, I grow my own vegetables and I cannot die because I have two young daughters, they will be left orphans." Kaki's eyes were filled with pain as she continued "As they are growing without any male member in this house, most of the men in this village have eyes on my daughters. I fear for their safety. They might be abducted, killed, or raped …that's my worst fear. I don't have money to get them married. They are not educated. God knows what will happen in the future" Sova felt her heart melting at Kaki's concern and condition. She knew she had to help the poor lady, she decided to speak to Nalin about them.

That night lying on the floor on a makeshift bed, Sova told Nalin about Rita Kaki's woes. Nalin was disturbed. He promised Sova he would do something for his sisters to help his aunt. The next day Nalin spoke to Rita Kaki. He asked about the allowance she was supposed to get and was surprised to know the village headman's treacherous attempt to pay her just half the sum being sent to her. "Don't say anything to him, Kaki pleaded, "he will make my life hell if he comes to know that I have told you this." Kaki was in tears. "If you really want to help me, please take my girls to the city, get them educated, and marry them. I can stay here but save my daughters" she pleaded. Nalin heard her plea and promised to do something about it. Sova came to him, seeing him troubled asked him what was he troubled about. Nalin told her that his plan was to take his sisters back to Calcutta and enroll them in school and arrange for a hostel facility for them. Sova was happy to hear his plan. They both went and informed Kaki and the girls about it. The girls looked at them as if their eyes would pop out in surprise. The girls had seen how the village headman use to come to their house, his eyes on them all the while. They were so frightened of him that they would dare not look at him when he would ask them to bring water or speak to them completely aware of their discomfort. They knew his intentions were very evil and every day their mother use to teach them how to protect themselves from the beast-like men of the village. They also knew their mother was being compromised for their safety. Rita Kaki teary-eyed thanked Nalin and Sova, blessing them for saving her daughters' lives. On the fourth day when Sova and Nalin were returning back to Calcutta, Sonali and Rupali too came back with them, they had a cotton cloth bag with a few torn clothes in it. Nalin knew he had taken up a great responsibility without his father's permission but then he could not have left his sisters to be exploited any further. Rita Kaki didn't shed tears as she saw her daughters board the bus, she felt relieved, and she knew from now she could sleep peacefully, as her daughters would be safe.

Nalin kept his promise to his aunt, enrolled them in a school for girls in Calcutta, and arranged the school hostel for them. Nalin did not want his father to interfere in this arrangement so he paid for all the expenses from his salary. Sova was touched by Nalin's effort, she realized he was so different and so humane by nature. This incident was deeply set in Sova's mind and now her father-in-law was planning the same punishment for her and her daughter in Boral.

"NO.... never.... I will never ever go to Boral", Sova spoke out loudly in the darkness of the night, she could imagine how her life would end if she ever went to Boral.

"I need an alternative plan", she told herself as she fell into a fretful sleep and had nightmares of being forced to go inside a dungeon....by strong animal-like hands.

The next few days she kept on thinking of her situation. Now she understood the sinister plan that had been hatched by her father-in-law and Ronit uncle. They wanted to take away her baby, Khuku, keep her and send Sova away to Boral to rot in poverty and destitution. The whole plan became so clear to Sova. The sweet talks of Aruna Aunty and the sympathy shown by them were all for a show, they wanted to emotionally weaken Sova into believing they meant to support her but in actuality, they wanted to take away her only reason to live – her daughter. No doubt both the brothers had reunited after a long time, because of this sinister plan. Sova wanted to dismiss these ill thoughts from her mind but she knew she was not wrong in her thoughts.

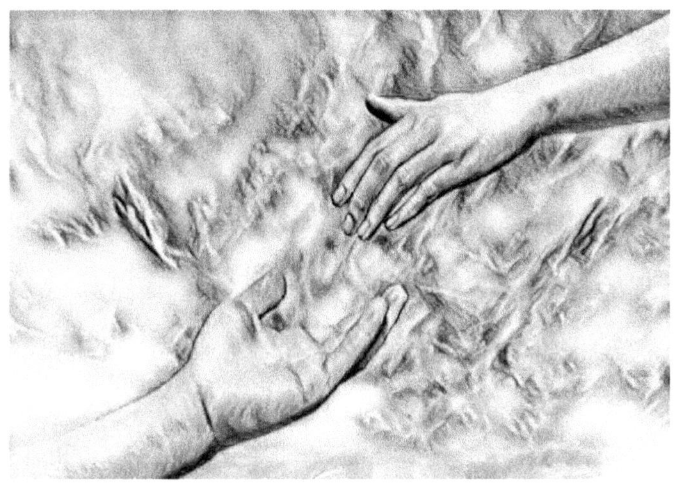

Chapter 12

The Plea for help

Maya Devi, Sova's mother was the second daughter of Mr Rajat Basu. Maya had always been the bold one in the family being the middle child, between two of her sisters, Meeta and Mina. When their mother died, Meeta took responsibility for the household and her young sisters. Maya was known by her family and neighbors to be that helpful girl who would extend her hand to help anyone who needed her. She was empathetic towards all, she would tend to the sick, take care of the animals, and help the less fortunate ones. She was most known amongst her sisters in their neighborhood.

Maya and her older sister Meeta were both married within two years gap, by the time they turned 14. Meeta went to Allahabad after her marriage, while Maya remained in Delhi. She was married to a Railway officer Subhas Mittra, she shifted to stay in the Railway colony on Barakhamba Road in Delhi. Maya's life was spent in social service most of the time. Whether it was Subhash's mother who fell ill in Patna, or some neighbor who could not afford treatment, or someone who needed to be looked after, it was always Maya who came to help. So Maya was always traveling, caring for the needful. Along with her young Sova traveled a lot.

When once Meeta fell ill, Sova's dad got a telegram from Allahabad. In the telegram was this message printed "Meeta ill. Come fast"

Maya spoke to Subhas and they agreed that Maya should go to help her elder sister. Sova was just 5 years old then. She too went to Allahabad, along with her mother.

The moment Maya saw her sister, she knew that Meeta's days were numbered. Tending so many ill people, she had learned to recognize the look of death. Meeta had recently given birth to her fourth son, in a span of 6 years of marriage. Her body was not able to cope with the pressure of repeated childbirths. She was anemic, her face looked pale white, and her eyes were sunken and not focused. She had not touched her baby boy since giving birth. The doctor had advised proper rest and nutrition and to avoid any kind of exhaustion. Maya took care of her sister and her kids and loved them like her own children. The boys got attached to Maya, she resembled their mother, whose deteriorating health was a matter of concern for all.

Meeta died. Maya stayed back to take care of her sister's family. Over a period of 2 years, Maya was tied to Allahabad. Sova was sent back to Delhi to be with her father and her grandparents, while Maya did everything any aunt would do and more for her sister's children. There was a twist in fate for one of the boys. The youngest of Meeta's boys was adopted by a rich family who didn't have children. This family had heard about the tragic death of Meeta and about her newborn baby. They had come to Meeta's husband and offered to adopt the child and bring him up. It turned out that they were related to Meeta's husband as well, so the adoption was done verbally, and no legal paperwork was carried out. Once this arrangement was complete, a caretaker cum cook was appointed by her brother-in-law. After settling them Maya returned back to Delhi, promising to keep coming back to take care of the family as and when needed. She kept her promise, slowly as the children grew older her visits reduced, but her brother-in-law was always in contact with her.

 "Maya, if you ever need me, please don't hesitate to ask. I will always be there for you" he had promised Maya, as the train left Allahabad, taking Maya back to Delhi. This had happened some 20 years back.

Maya had kept in touch with her brother-in-law and his family in Allahabad. She was in touch with her sister's sons, who loved her like their own mother, whom they had lost so early in life. In one of the letters Maya came to know Meeta's newborn who had been adopted by the rich family, had returned back to his father. When he turned 14, his adoptive parents had revealed to him his biological father's identity. The teenager was shocked at the revelation and had come to meet his father and elder brothers. Later he decided to return to his biological family because he wanted to know more about his own blood, he couldn't be with his adopted parents any longer. The adoptive parents had pleaded with him to change his decision, but the young boy had not budged. All the news was conveyed through letters to Maya and Maya guided them with her insights on various matters. All the boys had grown up managing their lives somewhat. The eldest son was working, the other three brothers were studying at Allahabad University.

As time passed, Maya continued her social work, though she did not travel much, but was helping in an orphanage near her house, on Barakhamba Road. It was a Tuesday, a day when she cooked for the children, any sweet dish they would demand. The children wanted rice pudding. Maya was cooking the pudding when Postman came with Sova's letter. "I thought you will be here so I came here", Hari, the Postman said, handing the blue inland letter to Maya. Hari had been delivering letters in that area for more than 15 years and knew everyone by name.

After serving the rice pudding to the children, Maya found a solitary place to sit and read the letter. She knew that Nalin was missing, she knew about the Jaan Bari prediction which Sova believed in with full faith, and she also knew how Sova was being tormented by her father-in-law for the loss of his son. Sova had been keeping her informed. Maya had suggested Sova to return back to Delhi and stay with them, she was their only child. They would be happy to have Sova and Khuku with them. But Sova had denied saying she needed to wait for Nalin to return back until he returns, she would not move from her in-laws' house.

But the letter Maya was reading, sent by Sova was not a regular one. She could sense the fear in Sova's letter. She had described the life of a widowed relative in the village, whom she had met. Sova had written, she would rather end her life than go to Boral village and stay. She had asked her mother to help her to flee from her father-in-law's house. "Ma, I cannot come to Delhi, he will know where to find me. Please find a place for me where my father-in-law can never find me or my daughter."

Maya read and then re-read the letter again and again, her mind busy finding a solution for her only daughter and her granddaughter. She knew the rules of the patriarchal society, Sova's father-in-law with his power and position would send her away to Boral village and forget her existence forever. Maya was busy thinking when suddenly a brilliant idea struck her. She took out an inland letter and started writing to someone.

Maya did not want to involve her husband in her mission to save her daughter because she knew Sova's father was a simple man, and would buckle under pressure if the situation arose. So, when she posted the letter, only she knew which city it was meant to go.

Chapter **13**

The Escape

It was Sunday evening, Rai Saheb had woken up after a deep siesta in the afternoon. On Sundays, he ate a very heavy meal. Apart from three types of fish curry, his favorite was poppy seed curry with white rice. An afternoon siesta is compulsory for all Bengali households after a heavy lunch, so every afternoon the Calcutta roads bear a deserted look as all the 'Babumosais' and their families sleep unmindfully after a heavy lunch. In the evening when Rai Saheb sat on the verandah, the servants brought him tea. Sipping his tea, he was feeling a bit uneasy, he couldn't understand the reason for feeling restless that evening. He dismissed his feelings and called for Ronit, his younger brother. Ronit came instantly.

"Did you call me, Dada", Ronit asked?

"Yes, I want you to take Sova and her child to Boral village by next week. I hope you have told her to pack her things" Rai Saheb had decided not to see Sova's face in his house anymore.

Ronit nodded and said, "Yes, I have seen her packing her things. I am sure she will be ready to leave soon".

Two days back, Ronit had seen her coming out of the house with a suitcase and had asked where was she going. Sova had said "Giving it for repair, the lock is jammed" Ronit had offered to help carry the suitcase to the shop which was a few yards away but Sova had politely declined saying she would do it herself.

"Has she agreed to give her daughter to you?" Rai Saheb asked.

Ronit answered grimly "No…she said that her daughter is her only reason to live and she cannot live without her daughter"

"Foolish woman" Rai Saheb hissed, "let her go to hell".

That night when Rai Saheb sat for dinner and was about to have his food, Dhanoi the maid came screaming with a troubled look on her face "Dada Babu…. Dada Babu…. Sova Bouma's room is dark…I went and switched on the light and no one was there, not even her things, clothes nothing is there…I think she has left the house"

Rai Saheb sat quietly for some time, then called his brother Ronit. Ronit came hurriedly.

"Go check Sova's room", he ordered his brother. Ronit returned after 5 minutes looking distressed. "I think she has left without informing us" Ronit spoke scared for his brother's reaction.

"Let her go", Rai Saheb roared in anger, "she will end up in a brothel. Mark my words"

Dhanoi, the other family members, and the servants who had gathered at the commotion cringed at Rai Saheb's harsh words. There was an emptiness in the house, which was so unbearable …no one knew how to react. They all knew that this news of Sova's disappearance would create a lot of shame for Rai Saheb in the near future and its repercussions would be felt by them, as Rai Saheb will continue to torture them for Sova's escape.

A month ago, when Ronit uncle had told Sova about the Boral village and her father-in-law's plan to shift her there, Sova had written to her mother for help. Sova's mother had replied two weeks later instructing her. "Go to Howrah station on 25th of June at 5:30 pm. There you will meet a man named Shishir in Platform No 1, near the ticket counter. The man will be wearing a white checked shirt and a pagri, a headgear worn by Sardars. He will call you by your nickname, the name I gave you when you were a baby. Once you are sure the man has your name right, go along with him and you will be safe. May the Almighty be with you". The letter had no other details. Sova had read the letter and then destroyed it.

On the 25th June afternoon, in the oppressive humid heat of Calcutta, when the whole house was in deep siesta; Sova had sneaked out with her daughter. She had packed her suitcase and had kept it at the Howrah station luggage room, two days back. She knew it would be difficult to leave the house with her daughter and luggage without being noticed. As she came out of the house with her daughter, she had a cloth bag where she carried her money and the brass idol of her god Bal Gopal, she climbed a rickshaw and was soon on her way to the bus station. She could feel her heart racing faster than the rickshaw wheels. She reached the bus station. Sova couldn't help looking around, she was frightened that people might recognize her and later inform Rai Saheb. She had worn a white saree, she had wiped off the red vermillion mark (sindoor) from her hair parting, which was a sign of a married woman. She was no longer going to wait for Nalin to come to her rescue. "Now if he wants to be with me, he has to come in search of me," Sova told herself as she pulled her white saree across her head covering her face as she climbed into the bus to Howrah station.

The journey seemed like a nightmare, Sova could almost feel so many unknown eyes searching for her, trying to track her down. She felt faint but something within her made her walk strongly towards the luggage room. She had carried with this procedure, two days back when she had come to deposit her luggage. The man in the locker room handed her, the suitcase. Sova took the suitcase in one hand and carried Khuku in her other hand and started moving towards Platform No 1.

Howrah station was like a sea of human beings. So many people were going to different destinations. Sova felt her throat parched, her vision was dazed. She walked towards the ticket counter. Just opposite the counter she placed her luggage and stood there waiting for the man, her mother had described, to appear. Her lips were moving in prayer as she looked around her anxiously.

It was almost 5 o'clock, she had been waiting at the station for almost 2 hours. She could hear Rai Saheb's voice screaming abuses at her…there was cacophony all around… suddenly she heard her name "Jhoka…Jhoka", Sova turned around and saw a Sardarji standing behind her calling her name, looking at her suspiciously. Sova looked at him and said, "Ami…. Ami Jhoka" (I am Jhoka). The man looked relieved. He was carrying a suitcase and a big rug sack.

"Ami Shishir", the Sardar ji spoke in fluent Bengali. Sova was relieved to hear his name. He gestured for her to move along with him. Soon they walked to Platform number 2 and climbed into the train bogey and Shishir located their seats. After placing their luggage safely under the seats, Shishir went to get water and food for the journey. Sova sat without breathing, fear of being caught and dragged back home was running in her mind. She was not sure, how long the train halted in the station but when she heard a slight chugging sound, she sat upright her mind registering the slight forward movement of the train. As the train moved slowly, she breathed out slowly…she had been holding her breath. Slowly the train started moving faster, Shishir came and sat opposite her. He too seemed quite uncomfortable. Khuku was in a playful mood, so Shishir got busy playing with the baby girl.

As the train caught speed, Sova could feel her breath normalizing. The cool wind soothingly blew her hair around. "Where are we going?", Sova asked Shishir enquiringly. Shishir looked surprised at her and answered "Allahabad". Sova was surprised too, but a small smile played on her lips. "You are Meeta Masi's son, isn't it?" Sova asked. Shishir smiled and nodded, he then removed his turban. "I am a theatre artist; I act in plays. I had come to buy costumes in Calcutta. I thought it would be a good idea to use this turban to disguise myself". Shishir seemed to enjoy the fact that he had pulled his stunt as a Sardar, quite well. As the train proceeded towards their destination Sova and Shishir talked about their mothers and how once Sova had been to Allahabad with her mother, she was barely five then. Sova tried remembering her last visit to Allahabad but she could not remember anything significant, except that the floor of their house was red in color.

Sova felt relief wash over her as the train rushed into the darkness, leading to her new life, towards a new light…in Allahabad.

Epilogue

Diary entry: 8 September 1949 10:30 pm

3 months have passed, and no one has come looking for us from Calcutta. I think I was able to escape successfully. But I need to be careful, Rai Saheb is a very powerful man. I need to stay low-key until I am sure, I cannot be tracked. I am not in contact with my mother, as I fear they will track me through her. Ma had instructed me not to contact her at all.

Diary Entry: 5th Nov 1949 6:30 pm

It was not easy to adjust to this new life but my uncle is a good man and so are my cousin brothers. Uncle has promised me that he would take care of and ensure Khuku will be educated, as it is my only wish. He has told me that Khuku will never miss her father's love in his house. I am so grateful to my uncle and my cousins.

16th January 1950 11:20 am

Khuku has been admitted to Jagat Taran School. My first step in educating my daughter begins from here. Nalin, wherever you are, I will fulfill your dream of educating our Khuku. Also, as you wanted, I have enrolled her as Lily Ghosh. I am still waiting for you to return. If you ever return back to your home and enter our room, I have left a clue for you to search for me. If we are destined to meet, we will meet before death parts us.

Sova had left a framed photo of goddess Kali on her bedroom wall…. on the photo frame over the glass sheet she had written "MAA" in her handwriting. Sova knew if Nalin ever returned and entered their room, he would see the photo frame with "MAA" written on it and would know where to look for her and his Khuku.

With this hope, she spent years caring for her uncle and his family. She took up her responsibility as an elder sister and made sure all her brothers were married and had their own family. She felt a bittersweet happiness as she saw her little girl grow up.

 Did Nalin ever return…like a floating leaf finds a temporary resting place… did Sova find her peace in Allahabad…did her life stop there…or was there another strong gust of wind waiting to float the leaf towards a different destination…

All these questions remain unanswered, because they are a part of another floating leaf story … 'LILY'.

www.ingramcontent.com/pod-product-compliance
Lightning Source LLC
Chambersburg PA
CBHW061139160726
48006CB00038B/2167